THE LIMIT

In the left-hand pocket he put three canisters, two of smoke and one of CS gas. He wiped the Luger of prints and stuck it into his belt, the butt concealed by the loose shirt. The flick knife with the six-inch blade he taped horizontally on to the tape that covered his stomach. He did it with care so that it would tug loose if he needed it.

He picked up the shotgun and felt its power. It was a beauty. An Ithica stakeout gun. They had a wicked way with weapons in the United States.

A five-shot, slide-action repeater with short barrel and pistol grip. It was fully loaded and he put a handful of extra 20-gauge cartridges into the right-hand patch pocket.

He put his hand through the slit pocket and took hold of the grip. The gun lay beneath the folds of the coat, ready and lethal.

Ready to go to the limit.

About the author

Peter Lacey has been a northern journalist for twenty-nine years and has worked as a crime reporter and feature writer. He married into a Blackpool family and his contacts include show-business personalities, seaside entrepreneurs and criminals. He now lives in Huddersfield.

The Limit

Peter Lacey

CORONET BOOKS
Hodder and Stoughton

The characters and situations in this book are entirely imaginary and bear no relation to any real person or actual happening.

First published in Great Britain in 1988
by Hodder and Stoughton Ltd

Coronet edition 1989

British Library C.I.P.

Lacey, Peter
The limit.
I. Title
823'.914[F]

ISBN 0 340 50064 6

Printed and bound in Great Britain for Hodder and Stoughton Paperbacks, a division of Hodder and Stoughton Ltd., Mill Road, Dunton Green, Sevenoaks, Kent TN13 2YA.
(Editorial Office: 47 Bedford Square, London WC1B 3DP) by Cox & Wyman Ltd., Reading.

For Virginia

Prologue

MARIO Rossetti stepped out of the back door of his nightclub and paused before walking towards the parked Mercedes.

It was one of those warm June nights that never get dark and that are filled with the promise of summer to come.

After the door had closed, he re-lit the King Edward cigar with a gold Dupont lighter. To him, even these narrow streets and cul-de-sacs reeked of optimism.

An extractor fan from the restaurant of the club whirred softly into action in the wall above his head.

Optimism and chips, he corrected. He laughed. If they ever bottled Blackpool and sold it as perfume it would come out as essence of chips.

The optimism was not just a warm night, it was real. Business was good and looking to get better, and life was full. Angie was a stay-at-home wife who was both loving and beautiful and his young family were a joy.

He refused to be depressed by the one problem that had arisen in the last two weeks. Problem? What problem? It could be dealt with; anything could be dealt with. No problem.

He exhaled smoke and felt for his keys as he stepped off the low pavement. The cul-de-sac was private and essential for staff parking in the season. The rear of the club and the chain mesh fence of a builder's yard made up its sides, and it ended in a brick wall. He had taken two steps when the Mercedes purred into life.

He stopped in surprise and was pinned in the beams of the headlights. Anger took over.

"Bastards!"

He began to run towards the car when the engine revved high and it came at him. Straight at him.

He dodged sideways but it caught him a glancing blow that threw him into the wall. His head smacked hard against the brick and he fell and rolled. His shoulders rested on the pavement and his head hurt like hell. His right leg was numb but it wasn't broken. His lightweight suit had ripped badly.

Jesus Christ, if he ever found out who they were he would have their balls.

And then they came back and he knew who they were.

The car had braked out on the street and now the reverse lights came on. The engine revved again – he could even see the tremble of the exhaust pipe – and it came hurtling backwards.

His mind froze with the inevitability and the horror.

"Jesus!"

The world had become two-dimensional: pain and blackness. The pain was intense and his only relief was the blackness of unconsciousness that intermittently covered him like a blanket. He attempted to crawl beneath the blanket but it kept slipping away. There were long stretches of time when he could do nothing but endure. His knowledge was confined to surviving the pain.

Awareness of a kind returned briefly. He was strapped down in an ambulance that swung wildly as it took corners. A white face floated in and out of vision above him. It was disembodied and did not look hopeful. He must be in a bad way. What the hell had happened?

The pain took over again but this time he managed to get beneath the blackness.

Impressions were jumbled and fleeting. Mainly there were chasms of nothing and jagged bursts of hurt. Then he felt a sharpness. He heard a calming voice and reached a plateau where the pain eased and he was able to rest.

He didn't dream but was vaguely aware of time passing, as if it were an endless grey corridor down which he floated. He acknowledged it passively until movement jostled his senses. The air smelled differently. He could smell. Where was he?

Voices. Quiet, anxious, reassuring.

He recognised the anxious one. Angie. What was Angie doing out at this time of night? She should be waiting for him at home. Who was looking after Bruno and Lucia?

"Just a few minutes, Mrs Rossetti. Don't tire him. He needs rest."

It was a Dr Kildare script. It couldn't be real life. But he knew he was in hospital. And suddenly, he remembered.

He felt there should be more pain – he remembered the pain – and fear. But his emotions were distanced. He must be drugged to the eyeballs. Balls. He remembered that, too. He had said he would have their balls. Anger was among the emotions lapping against the morphine.

"Mario? It's me. Angie."

She took hold of his hand and he concentrated his strength to squeeze her fingers. She must have felt it because she began to cry.

He loved her deeply but she was no good in situations like this. Situations like this needed the closed ranks of the family, but it was no longer there. It had broken up, drifted apart. He smiled to himself. He could feel the presence of his father, Big Bruno Rossetti, and his grandfather, Mario the Dealmaker. Surely he wasn't that close to death? If he was, he was in good company. The family was still there, all he had to do was call.

He tried to speak but although his lips moved, no sounds came out. Angie saw what he was attempting and leaned close.

"Yes, Mario. What is it?"

His concentration reactivated the pain despite the drugs but this time he managed to form the words.

"Get Toni."

He said it in a whisper that was almost inaudible and waited until he saw the understanding in his wife's eyes. Then he let himself slip back under the waiting blanket of sleep.

Chapter 1

MAUDIE discovered a Desmond Bagley, a Jack Higgins and a Gavin Lyall in the cardboard box of paperbacks.

Tommy the Tout had paid thirty bob for the books, a boilersuit, two jumpers and a pair of running shoes.

Tommy was careful with his money, which was why his second-hand shop was full of tat and his wallet full of tenners. Maudie, who looked after the retail side of things on a casual basis, knew that the shop was a sideline and that Tommy's main income came from other sources. He knew better than to ask what.

The pay he received wasn't much but it was cash in hand that supplemented his giro and the work was hardly demanding. He got to live in the bedsitter upstairs and to sit in a deckchair at the back of the shop, and had the pick of the paperbacks that came in.

He liked thrillers, though after half a lifetime with little to do but read, he found he had read most of them. It was a bonus to find three that he either had not read or had forgotten. He turned over the last book at the bottom of the box and struck gold – an Elmore Leonard.

For a moment he felt a surge of happiness. Elmore Leonard was the finest thriller writer he had ever read. Classier than the rest. A real find.

He put the box with the other paperbacks under the sign that said 15p each and returned to the deckchair. It was in its lowest reclining position and his back gave a twinge of complaint as he eased himself into it. It was a bit of a bugger getting in and out but the angle suited him because, with a cushion to support his head, he could hold the books far enough away for his eyes not to hurt.

He settled in and examined the covers, reading the blurbs on the back. The Jack Higgins now struck a chord so he put it under the chair as a last resort. Which of the others to read first? He would save the Elmore Leonard; it would be something to look forward to, a treat. He would start with the Desmond Bagley.

The cushion slipped when he reached into his cardigan pocket for the bag of Bombay bits he'd bought from the Paki shop next door, and he readjusted it, put a handful of bits in his mouth and opened the book. Halfway down the first page, someone stepped into the open doorway and blocked the sunshine.

He raised his eyes without moving his head and got a surprise. She was as classy as an Elmore Leonard. In her thirties and beautifully put together. He could see that because the summer dress she wore was cream silk. The sun shone through it to provide a silhouette that made the bits catch in his throat.

He coughed.

What the hell was she doing down Brick Lane? If the shop had been up Hampstead she could have confused it for trendy junk, but this was Tower Hamlets and Tommy the Tout's emporium couldn't be mistaken for anything other than what it was.

The cough made her turn towards the sound and she removed a pair of tinted glasses. She obviously hadn't seen him when she had come in and he was embarrassed that she might discover he had been looking through her dress.

He put the books on the floor and tried to get up as though it didn't hurt. Vanity, at his age. He stood up and the Bombay bits scattered on the floor. He ignored them and walked towards her.

"Yes, madam? Can I help you?"

Christ, he sounded like a floorwalker at Harrod's. But

she was a madam. Certainly not a luv. Even better looking, now he was closer, than he had first thought.

She hesitated and looked past him into the darkness of the shop.

"There's nobody else." He smiled. "I'm afraid I'll have to do."

At least smiling was something he could do with confidence. His teeth had been well looked after and even improved, at not inconsiderable expense, by some of the finest dental surgeons in the prison service.

"I'm sorry." She smiled back and it was a bonus far greater than hunting for paperbacks. "Are you Tommy Ainsworth?"

"Sorry. The Tout is out." He grinned to show it was a joke and she grinned back. "He's only here first thing for an hour or two. Can I take a message?"

She was looking at him more closely and he leaned back imperceptibly to focus his own gaze. The gold was flash but impressive. Among the chains around her neck was one that held a small gold horn of plenty. It stirred a distant memory.

"Actually, it's not Mr Ainsworth I'm looking for. I'm looking for Mordecai Morgan. I was told he was an associate of his."

"I'm Mordecai Morgan. Although most people call me Maudie, these days."

She tried to keep the disappointment from showing but he saw it in her eyes. He needed only a nudge and he would remember. He began to sweat because he was almost sure he would not want to remember.

The accent was not London. It was an accent that had been around, travelled, but that still had a touch of the north. She held out a card and he remembered.

"You gave me this some years ago. A long time ago."

Too long ago?

The card brought back memories. It said: Mordecai

Morgan, Demolition, and gave a number at the Bow end of Roman Road.

He had first had them printed as a joke but the joke stuck and helped his reputation thirty years before. This must have been one of the last he had had printed and given out. Sixteen, seventeen years ago?

He remembered. And he wished he hadn't.

"I'm Toni Rossetti," she said. "You knew my grandfather."

He nodded.

"The Dealmaker," he said.

He felt old and foolish and did not want to ask why she had traced him after all this time. It would not be for a reunion party. There could only be one reason.

"You found me with that?" he said, giving her the card back.

"Yes." She smiled, as if she had come to terms with her disappointment. "It wasn't difficult. You're still well known."

That, at least, was true. The East End cherished its characters. If it had nothing else it had pride in its identity and folk lore. Old ladies still talked of Ronnie and Reggie with affection. "Lovely boys. Thought the world of their mum."

"It's been a long time, Toni."

He held his hands away from his sides as if to say look at me. He wished he had shaved that morning and had washed properly and wondered if she could smell last night's drink seeping from his pores. Sometimes, he could smell it himself.

She looked round again, but this time as a diversion, to avoid getting to the point. She had, perhaps, realised there no longer was a point.

"Do you work here?"

"I help out. Tommy's an old friend. From racetrack days."

She nodded and looked away again.

"Why are you here?"

He had to ask it. He had never tried to avoid the truth, even when it hurt. Even now.

She met his eyes.

"I need help. You once said . . ."

"I know."

They looked at each other sadly.

"I thought perhaps you could advise me."

It was a nice shift in emphasis. A face saver for them both. And perhaps he could.

"If I can."

"Is there somewhere we can talk? Maybe go for a drink?"

He would have loved to have gone with her for a drink, to have walked into the pub with a classy lady on his arm and have everyone stare. It would have revived his reputation. But not looking like he did.

"We can talk here," he said, and walked past her to lock the shop door and change the sign.

He also had no money to take her for a drink. He had 46p in his pocket.

He led the way to the office at the rear. It held an old-fashioned rolltop desk, two dining-room chairs and a Formica table with an electric kettle, mugs and a jar of cheap instant coffee. He pointed at the jar as she sat down but she shook her head.

"No thanks."

"I don't blame you. It's bloody awful."

Perhaps they should have stayed in the shop. The atmosphere was close in here and he became worried about his body odour. He opened the back door into the yard and remained standing, staying as far away as was polite.

"You were a lovely girl, Toni. You've become a beautiful woman."

She laughed.

"Hard work and bad marriages have kept me trim."

"Marriages?" He emphasised the plural.

"Two. One here and one in America. I'm currently single and intend to stay that way."

"How long did you live in America?"

"I still do. Portland, Oregon. I came back to help my brother, Mario. He's in hospital."

Maudie raised his eyebrows.

"What's wrong? Something serious?"

"He was run down by a car outside his club. Deliberately. That's why I'm here."

He pulled the other chair towards him and sat down.

"You'd better tell me all about it."

Chapter 2

ANTONIETTA Rossetti hadn't hesitated when she received the call. Within thirty-six hours she had handed over the running of the beauty salon and dress shop to her manageress, grabbed six thousand dollars in readies and made the connection from Portland to Seattle for the Polar flight to Heathrow.

Angie hadn't made a lot of sense on the telephone but then Angie rarely did. Her helplessness was part of the reason why Mario loved her so much. When Toni finally arrived in Blackpool, other things didn't make sense either.

She had come dashing home on a Pan Am white charger to make everything right for her kid brother and discovered that she couldn't. Mario was out of intensive care but would be in hospital for some time and Uncle Emilio had done a runner to Malta, leaving problems well beyond the scope of normal man-management or bent accounting.

Three days later, the problems had got even bigger. She needed help. The sort of specialised help that wasn't available in Blackpool.

The police theory was that joyriders had run over Mario by accident when he disturbed them. They had abandoned the car, undamaged, five miles out of town. She used it to drive to London.

She had come alone and hadn't told anyone where she was going. It had been a long shot and it had come off – sort of. Perhaps she had made the trip to fool herself into believing activity was the same as action. Perhaps she had been living too long on American dreams for reality to register.

But she had found Maudie and she had rehearsed the story in her mind during the drive south. He might still have contacts and he might still be able to help. And, when it came to the bottom line, he was all she had.

She began to tell him and once she started talking it became a relief to unburden herself, to be able to confide in someone else.

"You know the family, Maudie. We've always been close, always had respect. It was earned through three generations. Grandfather, my father and now Mario. We've been in Blackpool since 1934. Now somebody wants us out."

She paused, took from her handbag a packet of St Moritz and the gold Dupont lighter that had been a present from her brother, and lit a cigarette. Maudie pushed across a saucer to use as an ashtray.

"They're called Dyson Enterprises. Two brothers, Eric and Steven. Eric was an accountant in Manchester. He looked after the books for a string of strip joints, drinking clubs and dives around Ancoats and Moss Side. Neighbourhoods that are less than salubrious. He was involved in prostitution and drugs without getting his fingers dirty. He made a lot of contacts into the bargain.

"Steven Dyson is two years younger, in his mid thirties. Flasher than his brother. Upper-class flash. A university dropout who went to Morocco or somewhere. When he got back to Manchester he cut his hair, bought a suit and went into public relations.

"They teamed up and went to Blackpool three years ago and bought partnerships in two businesses. Sedgwick's betting shops and Bateman's bingo halls. Within months, their partners sold out and retired to the sun.

"Leo Sedgwick and Arnold Bateman were fixtures in the town, like the Tower Circus. They were not retiring types.

Leo left after someone set fire to his Rolls-Royce. Arnold put minders in his bingo halls but someone put his minders in hospital and suddenly he couldn't get replacements."

"Police?"

"The Dysons are respectable and clever. The violence is non-attributable. Eric is a Rotarian. They support charities. Steven's leading a drive to raise funds for the football club. They get their pictures in the local paper every other week, doing good. They're popular. They make money and they spend it.

"Last year they bought a run-down pub and have turned it into a fun bar called The Life of Riley. It mints money. Blackpool likes success and they're successful. They also haven't challenged any of the big companies. They've concentrated on small independents. Mario is the biggest they've tackled."

"How?"

She took a long drag on the cigarette before replying, taking comfort from the menthol hit at the back of her throat.

"When my father died twenty-one years ago, he left a public house, a nightclub and two bingo halls. I was sixteen, Mario was fourteen. He was too young to take over and I was never considered. I was a girl. Uncle Emilio ran things for four years. He meant well but he had no head for business. By the time Mario was eighteen, we had lost the pub and one of the halls. Emilio got a twenty per cent shareholding of Rossetti Entertainments as a payoff and Mario rebuilt.

"Mario now has three halls, a nightclub, a share in a seafront hotel and bar, and the long-term lease of a prime site that has four shops and cafes, all bringing in rent. He's done well. He looked after Uncle Emilio, too. He let him run the bingo halls. But Emilio always had a weakness – gambling. And that's how the Dysons moved in.

"Emilio was always a mad punter. Years ago my father

had to bail him out when he got in over his head. It was well known around town and, ever since, when Emilio gambled or had a bet it was strictly cash. The Dysons must have known. They gave him an account. It didn't take long before he owed them fifteen thousand pounds."

Maudie whistled.

"Then they extended his credit. Another fifteen. They took his shares in the business as security. He signed documents and when he'd lost the extra, they kept the shares. They became twenty per cent partners of Rossetti Entertainments. That's the bingo halls and the club."

"Is it legal?"

"As legal as it needs to be. They have Emilio's books for the halls. The ones for the taxman and the other set. But they're not content with twenty per cent. They want the lot. They made Mario an offer and threatened to make the books public if he didn't sell. Mario turned them down flat. The bingo would be no good to them if it was straight. You need the bunce off the top to make it worthwhile. He offered them forty grand for the shares back and called their bluff."

"And they ran him down?"

"With his own car outside the club. He's got broken legs and internal injuries." She shrugged. "They say he's comfortable. He'll be all right."

"Are you sure it was the Dysons who ran him down?"

"They had it done. They have more muscle than they need for running their business. Some of it professional. I made enquiries. They have a team of persuaders run by two thugs from Manchester. Paul Unsworth and Carl Curtis. Curtis served five years for manslaughter.

"Blackpool has always been hard. You have to be hard to survive on the Golden Mile during Glasgow Fairs, but that's mindless violence. You can cope with that. When it's planned it becomes frightening."

She stubbed out the cigarette and remembered the last three days.

"I went to see them. To make them a fresh offer to get the shares back, before I was convinced they were responsible. It was all very civilised, in the boardroom at their offices at The Life of Riley. They said they were sorry about Mario's accident, turned me down and insisted they wanted to buy Mario out. The intimidation started later.

"There was trouble at Dolly's, that's Mario's nightclub, when four heavies tried to wreck the place. I was threatened in a car park." She laughed, and wondered if it sounded brittle. "It was intended to show me that the streets at night are not safe for a woman alone." She could still taste the revulsion of the encounter. "And they sent this to Mario."

She reached in her handbag and took out a photograph that she gave to Maudie.

"Don't tell me," he said. "This is Mario's wife and kids?"

"That's right. A polaroid snapshot in the park. Angie probably never even knew it had been taken. It arrived at the hospital in an envelope. No message, no threat, just the photograph."

"What did Mario say?"

"He said he might sell. His wife and kids are his world."

"What did you say?"

"I got him to send Angie and the kids to stay with Mother. She married again and lives in Rimini. They went yesterday. Then I asked him to give me more time to work something out."

"And you came here, looking for Clint Eastwood?"

She lit a second cigarette.

"No. I came for help. Any help you can give, Maudie."

Chapter 3

MAUDIE regretted being flippant. While she had been talking his stomach had become light and empty. A nervous feeling without the nerves. One that he had once been used to. The remark about Clint Eastwood had been self-derogatory, not a criticism of her hope.

"I'm sorry, gel."

He sat back in the chair and wondered how to let her down lightly. Her story had been clear and well told. The Dysons sounded like middle-class ponces who could buy muscle without commanding its respect. They wouldn't have lasted long thirty years ago. But now? What did he tell Toni? He began to reminisce out loud.

"It's changed down here, since the old days. The loyalties, the old-time values, have gone. They went with the Krays. When Jack Spot and Billy Hill ran things, you could trust somebody's word. Ronnie and Reggie changed all that. They enjoyed violence too much. No honour, just violence."

He came back to the present.

"But that doesn't help you, does it?"

He thought aloud some more.

"The lads round here are no use. There are plenty of tearaways, none with nous. You could try the Italians in Clerkenwell. But that'd be no good. If they were invited to a deal up north they'd stay." He shook his head. "You'd be better off praying for a miracle in St Peter's Italian church than get involved with them. No disrespect to Italians. Just the Clerkenwell mob.

"What you need is a Jack Spot or Billy Hill. They could handle violence when they had to. They were prepared to go the limit. They lasted so long because they were clever. They knew when to be hard and they knew when to fix things. They were dealers. Like your grandad. That's why Jack liked him. Your grandad. That's why both Jack and Billy retired when they saw things changing. Retired. Not banged up in top security or Rampton. Retired."

Toni remembered, too, as he talked. The family legend of how Grandfather Mario had met Jack Spot Comer, the gangland ruler of the West End, at a boxing match in London.

Spot had been loud and bombastic. Grandfather Mario, without knowing who he was, had finally had enough. He had got to his feet, drawn himself up to his full five feet three inches and, punctuating his words with the fat cigar between his fat fingers, had told Spot to shut his mouth.

Spot had liked his honest bull-terrier aggression. Instead of taking offence he had invited him to dinner. Grandfather had accepted and their friendship had been casual but lasting. It had continued after Grandfather died.

The gang leader had visited Blackpool only once. His business had been elsewhere, Haydock or Manchester racetrack. Toni had been a child but she remembered his visit to the house. It was years later that she discovered who and what he was.

He had arrived with three men, one of them Maudie. The visit had been brief. He had left a small suitcase, which her father had locked in a safe, and collected it the next day. Her father had not attempted to look inside.

She had been nineteen when she next met Maudie at Brian London's 007 Club in Blackpool. The doorman had asked her to sign in a guest. The guest had been Maudie and when he read her name as he signed the book after her, he had introduced himself.

Toni had been intrigued at meeting an associate of a famous underworld figure who was living proof that the family legend was true. She had been impressed with his quiet but totally assured manner. His age hadn't mattered, she had simply categorised him as beyond her scope of romantic interest, and he had behaved with an old-world courtesy that had charmed her but been a deterrent to casual boyfriends.

They had met three times during the course of the week, each time at the 007 Club, and once they had gone for a meal at an Italian restaurant afterwards. Other people had been present, but in a temporary way, flitting in and out of their company. His mystery had fascinated her and she had never discovered what he was doing so far from London.

The last night he had given her the card and said, "If you ever need me, give me a call."

He had said it quietly, with his usual understatement, but his meaning had been clear. She had treasured the card.

It was one of the last he had given out. Seventeen years ago? It must be eighteen.

He had enjoyed being with her during that strange week in the northern seaside resort. He absentmindedly felt in his cardigan pocket for Bombay bits and was glad he didn't have any when he realised what he was doing.

The card and the week had been a late flourish as his career of crime went into decline. A career that had started so well, too. Ten years of being a somebody with Jack Spot.

After the war, Jack and Billy Hill had run the West End between them – two blokes with bottle. When they had a major disagreement they settled it themselves. August, 1954. The papers called it The Battle of Frith Street when Jack and Billy went at each other with knives in the streets of Soho. One against one, instead of a gang war. How would the Dysons have made out in such company?

A year later, the Krays went to work for Spotty. The twins from Vallance Road had a fearsome reputation. Maudie knew them, of course. They shared the same heritage of Vicky Park, Tubby Isaac's pie and eel stall, Bloom's, and graduation from Shepton Mallet military nick. And it wasn't long before Jack and Billy stepped aside for the new generation.

Maudie didn't join the Krays' Firm until 1961, by which time they had Esmeralda's, their first uptown bar. Very respectable. Very tiara and tonic. Maudie stayed down Bethnal Green Road and ran a spieler. He also performed other services. Ronnie had an understanding with the Glasgow gangs, and Maudie made four trips north. Loch Lomond had been the most memorable.

He and Dempsey Wogan had arrived there very early one morning, mist over the water, birds just waking, the air fresh enough to make you drunk. It had been bloody beautiful, the first and only time nature had really moved him. Then he had got on with the job and kneecapped a Jock. Reggie had called it a reciprocal favour. Maudie didn't remember the Jock but he had always remembered Loch Lomond.

Then the twins had got too big and Ronnie began to believe he was Al Capone. He walked into the bar of The Blind Beggar and shot George Cornell in the head. That was the moment Maudie realised Ronnie had gone potty, the moment Maudie got out. It wasn't healthy to be around any more. Friends as well as enemies disappeared. The end came when the twins stabbed to death harmless Jack the Hat to prove how tough they were. They were arrested. Maudie, and a large section of the East End, were relieved when they were put away.

Maudie had lost his enthusiasm by watching Ronnie's totally mindless violence. He had gone looking for that one-off job that could set him up for life. Instead, he had almost got life.

Now he was serving out his time in the Tout's shop, and that might not be for ever. Business was not exactly brisk and he felt it would not be long before the premises were sold out to another all-hours Paki shop or curry house. Maudie's next stop could be down the road at the dossers' crypt at Spitalfields Christ Church.

"What were you doing in Blackpool? When we met at the nightclub?" Toni asked.

He grinned.

"I was taking a holiday. Because of the interest of the Metropolitan Police. A wages snatch."

"Did they catch you?"

"Not for that. But they got me for the next. I took a holiday in Spain that time – no disrespect to Blackpool – but got fed up after three weeks. I had an overwhelming urge for light and bitter." He grinned again. "They lifted me on my first night back. Full of light and bitter. I was away three years."

"Away?"

"Banged up. Prison."

"What did you do when you came out?"

"More of the same. I was a mug. A warehouse job first. That went all right. Then another wages van. Securicor had improved. It went wrong. Bloody wrong. I was caught two days later and got a ten stretch. I did seven."

"God. Seven years? It seems for ever."

"Nothing's for ever. Especially when you get older."

"Since then?"

"Since then I've done nothing. I didn't want to go back inside, you see. I was fifty-six when I came out last time. Another heavy pull and I'd have been in for what was left of my life. I now wonder why I tried so hard to stay out. When you get past fifty, life's an express train." He tilted his head back and looked at the ceiling. "Where did it all go?"

"I'm sorry."

"No need to be sorry. I had good times. More than most. But I crammed them all in at the beginning and left none for my old age. It's me that's sorry. For giving you that card. I was forty-five and pretending I was still in my prime. I was being Jack the lad. Showing off. I shouldn't have."

"I'm glad you gave it to me." She said it with a determined effort to be cheerful. "That card has been through Europe and across America. I've impressed countless numbers of people with it and frightened a few that got on my nerves."

He chuckled, then became thoughtful again.

"Look, Toni. You took me by surprise, turning up out of the blue. Give me time to think. Maybe I can come up with someone, something. Are you staying in town?"

"I haven't checked in anywhere, but yes. I'll be staying overnight. I have to go back tomorrow. I have a dinner date with Steven Dyson. It was the price of a truce. I said we should talk and the intimidation stopped."

"Can I see you tonight?" he said. "If I don't come up with anything, at least I can buy you a drink." He would have to dip into the till but the Tout wouldn't mind when he explained. He shrugged. "You caught me at a bad time. I'll be more presentable tonight."

"Sure. We'll have a drink and I'll buy you dinner. A business dinner," she added, to stifle protests. "Part of the consultancy fee." She opened her handbag and palmed banknotes, then held out her hand. "Take it, Maudie. You're a professional with expert advice to offer. In my business, advice is paid for."

She pushed the money into his hand and walked back into the shop before he could return it. He followed. At the front door she looked back.

"I'll pick you up at eight. Here?" He nodded. "Think of a good Indian restaurant to take me to. As I recall, you grumbled all the way through stuffed peppers and spaghetti eighteen years ago."

When the door opened and the sun once more burst in, he could see her silhouette through the dress again. It was just for a moment, before his eyes misted.

He realised, with surprise and despair, that he was crying.

Chapter 4

A HUNDRED pounds.

She had given him a hundred pounds.

The money lay alongside him on the bed. He had locked up the shop and gone upstairs. He had felt unable to face either Desmond Bagley or second-hand customers for the rest of the day.

He had a lump in his throat. It was one of those expressions that sounded silly, that people use when they couldn't make words fit. But he really did have a lump in his throat.

The back of his eyes still prickled with the tears but they had only lasted until he became aware of them. They had been replaced by a feeling of emptiness.

Who was he kidding? He wouldn't be able to come up with anyone or thing that might help Toni Rossetti. He had been out of circulation too long and the power now lay with the Maltese, the Italians, the Chinese and the gangs over the river. The London crime barons were settled in respectability on the coast, at Southend and Leigh-on-Sea. Even the Jew Crew commuted from the seaside.

His own reputation in the East End had been reduced to that of a character. Young tearaways gave him a nod of acknowledgment and the current faces had a joke and bought him a drink. At least they still treated him with esteem and not as a dosser.

A hardman in his day – and no one knew better than he did that his day was past.

Years before he had paid the same dues to his seniors. When he was one of Jack's top boys and, later, when he had worked for the Krays.

People had moved to give him space at the bar and he had made a point of being polite to the hardmen of a previous generation. They were fellow tradesmen and if they were over-the-hill, well, it happened to everyone sooner or later, if you didn't cop the big one first.

So he had bought them a drink and exchanged a word that let the others know – the petty thieves and the straights – that they were different. That the willingness not simply to face violence, but to charge it head on, made them a breed apart.

The few words, the few beers, the respect he had given all those years before had been payments in a pension fund. And now he was a pensioner hardman, gone soft with age and drink.

He picked up the money. The notes were crisp and new. He was sick at himself for accepting them. His pride had wanted to refuse but his poverty had made his reactions lethargic. It was a long time since he had had a hundred pounds.

The situation was ludicrous. He had only met Toni Rossetti on a handful of occcasions and that had been a lifetime ago. It was his fault that she had built false expectations.

He had let her believe that he had been more important than he was and that Jack Spot Comer had still been a man to be feared. By then, Spot had retired to sell furniture and he had been a member of the Krays' Firm for five years.

But, at the time he met her and impressed her, it had been safer to talk about Spotty than the twins. People who talked about the twins got their legs blown off in 1967.

He got off the bed and looked at himself in the full-length mirror on the wardrobe door.

Christ. What must the girl have thought, seeing him like this? At least he could improve his image before he saw her again. Maybe salvage something, like pride.

He went down to the shop and took from the rack the dark blue suit that he had noticed when it first came in. It was nice gear, hardly worn and it almost fitted. The style was conservative and hadn't dated and the material had a fine stripe.

He tried it on in front of the wardrobe. The jacket was all right but the trousers were an inch too big at the waist and two inches too long. He got out the Quality Street tin that held needles, cotton, buttons and the paraphernalia of sewing, and got to work. Needlecraft had been a useful prison skill.

When he was satisfied with his tailoring, he shaved and went out and bought underclothes, a white shirt and a pair of black shoes. He was careful with the money and spent twenty-six pounds, realising only after he had left the shoe shop that his priorities, apart from the price, had included toes for kicking. Old habits.

It had been a long time since he had actually taken a proper bath. He had got into the habit of having a whore's bath – a body wash at the kitchen sink – when it became necessary, and sometimes not even then. It needed a special reason to take a proper bath, and there had been few of them in his life in recent years. But now he had a reason.

The bath was grubby but he ran the water deep and hot and made it sudsy with half a packet of Daz. He soaked in it and imagined that it made his back feel better. When he got out and towelled himself dry, he touched the memories on his body for the first time in an age.

A knife wound in his left side, razor cuts on his left arm and right shoulder, and the bullet scar on his left thigh.

He had packed his early life with good times, he had told Toni. They had been, too. There was no other feeling to match the exhilaration of battle. It may have been a madness but it had been a special kind of madness.

People had stepped aside, women had been available, he had always had money and friends. He had never been able to understand straights: how they could motivate themselves to get up and go to work each day, be content to settle down with a girl from the next street and bring up a brood of kids.

A life of snot and hire purchase had never appealed to him except, perhaps, in the middle period of his seven stretch. He had wondered then, briefly and in depression, whether it might not have been better to have had a family.

He had come out of the depression and realised that, for him, a family would not have worked. He was a loner, he had told himself, who lived on the edge. He would always be a loner.

That had certainly been true since his release. Prison had sapped his self-belief. He had served his sentence, one day at a time, the only way to survive, and had come out to find that life could no longer be lived the same way. It was a young world and he was fast approaching old age and did not know how to stop it happening.

The speed of time passing frightened him. He could no longer live on the edge for the fear of returning to prison. He had dropped into apathy and a world of old paperback books for self-protection. He had been hiding from reality for eight years.

He ironed the creases out of the new shirt and dressed with care. The only thing from the past that he wore was a dark blue knitted tie. It was silk and still bore the Bond Street label of its maker.

He checked his appearance again in the wardrobe mirror. The improvement was dramatic and he couldn't stop smiling self-consciously at himself and winking at his embarrassment. But there was still something wrong. His hair. It was grey, wispy and too long.

There was time to get it cut.

He straightened his shoulders and felt the tingle in his stomach. Empty and light.

There was also time to see the Chinaman.

Chapter 5

THE hotel room was an oasis. She felt she had been centre stage for the last seventy-two hours. Tiredness had hit her in debilitating waves that retreated as soon as she resigned herself to sleep. The 6,000-mile trip always wrecked her internal body clock and events had added to the pressure.

But now she had found Shangri-la and it came with en-suite bathroom, telephone, TV and shag-pile carpet.

She undressed and caught sight of her reflection in the full-length mirror on the wall.

Not bad for a mature woman in her late thirties. She knew she looked good; she had taken care of herself. Of course, missing out on childbirth had helped. She smiled wrily at the mirror.

A long hot shower washed away the anxiety of the drive down to London. Afterwards she lay on the bed in a towelling robe.

She felt safely isolated in the amorphous womb of the hotel room, safe to reflect on her enforced homecoming and three days of upheaval, shock, distress and anger.

Three days.

Everybody had said that if her father hadn't died so young, things would have been different. Perhaps they would, perhaps not. Her father's death had changed a lot of things for her and her brother.

When Big Bruno Rossetti died of a heart attack at forty-two, he had a small mansion, a healthy empire and a lot of respect. He was strong on family and he protected his own. His dying words to his wife were the combination of the second safe, the one containing the undeclared cash and the real set of books.

His funeral was an Italian wake. He lay in state in an open, silk-lined casket, in the oak-panelled study for three days and nights. The women wailed, the men were stern and moist-eyed. They spoke fine words over the coffin and Toni heard them all.

For most of the daylight hours she sat by her father's side and held his cold hand. The imprint of her fingers was in his flesh when they finally screwed down the lid.

She began to cry for the first time when the cars arrived for the funeral. While he had been here, in the house, it was simply a pageant of which he was a part. But the coffin lid was final.

There were forty-two cars in the funeral cortège and more at the church and cemetery. All the shops on the main road were closed and their blinds drawn in respect.

Respect. It had been a hard act to follow for her brother.

But once Mario had come of age and asserted himself, he had earned his own respect. He had done well. Until he had been put into hospital. Seeing him there had been a shock.

He was a big man, but being prone and immobile had made him seem smaller. That first day back, she still thought he had been the victim of a hit and run, and found his story of what had really happened almost too incredible to believe. She had pacified him and promised to sort everything out. After all, what were big sisters for?

If she had been born a boy, Mario's empire would have been her empire. Now she had it by default, at least for the time being. Her first priority had been to make sure it continued to run smoothly.

Jimmy Docherty had worked for Rossetti Entertainments

for ten years and been club manager at Dolly's for the last three.

Mario valued him because he was loyal and he was not greedy. He was paid good wages which he augmented with his own fiddles. It was a balance many managers did not always appreciate and, as a result, got a thumping or the sack or both. Greed could be unrewarding and painful.

Dolly's had a disco, cabaret room, dining areas and lounge bars, spread over two floors of what had been a co-operative laundry. It was on its third name change. On a Friday or Saturday night in the season, it would be heaving with locals and holidaymakers, but at eleven thirty in the morning it was occupied only by the cleaners.

Toni visited him in his first-floor office on her first day back. He was a small, compact Scot with dark hair that was greying at the temples although he was only in his mid thirties. He wore a pale blue shirt and slacks and a pink sweater. A fine gold chain was round his neck and a chunkier one on his wrist. The other wrist held a slim gold watch on a bracelet and he wore two rings – a large ruby and the obligatory gold sovereign. His walnut tan gave the gold lustre. The flashy opulence suited him.

They talked about Mario and about the business.

"You'll be able to keep things running, won't you, Jimmy?"

"No problem. Tighter than ever. Staff sometimes get sticky fingers if the boss is away. I won't let them."

It was an assurance that he wouldn't take advantage of Mario's absence, but she had known that already. Jimmy Doc was sharp but, like many Scots, he was very strong on honour. Besides, once back, it wouldn't take Mario long to spot major discrepancies.

"Will you be able to look after the bingo as well?"

"I dare say."

"Do you know the managers?"

"Not well, but I know them. Malcolm Batty is at Dixon

Road, Peter the Pole has Talbot Road and Fat Gerard is still at South Shore. They all need watching but Gerard's been there for years. Anyway, you know Gerard."

"Yes. I know Gerard."

Fat Gerard had always been fat. He had first been a manager fifteen years before but hadn't been able to keep his hands out of the prize bingo money. The prize bingo was the non-accountable income.

Playing card bingo for cash prizes was, in the main, tightly regulated and traceable. It was the games for prizes in between that provided undeclared profits.

Cram in as many games as possible for swag that ranged from digital watches with a twenty-four-hour guarantee to Taiwanese blankets, and make money.

The prizes were well-packaged and displayed, the more lavish requiring accumulated wins to be claimed. They were bankrupt stock, flood damaged, job lots, misplaced deliveries. They cost flumpance but they looked enticing.

In the early days, the system had been to collect the prize bingo money in a bucket. Gerard had thought it was Christmas every day until Mario noticed his expensive jewellery and the diminishing returns. He had been sacked and Mario had changed the system. Over the years he had been re-employed and sacked for a variety of reasons. But at least he had learned his lesson about taking too much as his unofficial bonus.

Jimmy Doc said nothing to suggest he knew of any Dyson connection with Mario's injuries and Toni did not enlighten him. She needed to ensure the smooth running of the business before moving into those murky waters.

"I don't intend to bother you, Jimmy. This is your turf. But I need to know now what sort of cash flow I can expect. And I don't mean what the accountant knows about."

Jimmy nodded.

"The earners are door money, bandits and booze. Weekends there are a thousand punters a night. They pay four quid to get in. Weekdays and Sundays it's fewer numbers, two quid, less take. We cream a grand a week.

"There are three bandits. They're licensed, legal and metered. The meters are turned off one night a week and that brings two fifty. The booze is bought two ways. From a declared supplier with recorded accounts, the rest cash and carry. We make four hundred on a litre case of spirits and we don't need lead in the optics. Booze is about eight hundred a week. There's some off food, too.

"Mario takes about two grand a week in readies from the club, plus a grand from the halls. His policy is don't be greedy. That way, you don't get caught. Even by the Vatman."

Toni smiled and remembered their father's advice. Always take the same percentage. If it's a good week, don't be tempted to take more. If it's a bad week, still take the same. And leave the shillings and pence. Never round up the take.

"Apart from the cream, how's business?"

"Legit? Never better. We make money that way, too."

Talking money had made her feel more optimistic. At least Rossetti Entertainments would continue to function despite her brother's hospitalisation, and her presence would be a deterrent to any middle management who might be tempted to overstep the accepted bounds of dishonesty.

But she still hadn't taken the Dyson brothers seriously. Not until she had learned from independent sources how they had moved into town and after she had met them herself, in their offices, and their hired help in a dark car park.

It had been that last experience, more than anything, that had sent her looking for the Mordecai Morgan of yesteryear with a burning desire to fight back.

Chapter 6

DISCOVERING the truth about the Dysons had started with Stuart and Ruth Shapiro.

Stuart had been a family friend for more than twenty years. At one time, in her teens, they had been flirtatious without anything ever happening. Instead, she had introduced him to her best friend, and he had married her.

He was a big but gentle man. His father had unsuccessfully attempted to push him into a profession but he had quit as a trainee surveyor after less than a year and got a job painting the Tower. It was steady work, like the Forth Bridge. Once it was finished, the gang started all over again. Then his father relented, gave him a stake, and he went on the markets.

He had become a market baron. He had knitwear stalls in four permanent markets in Blackpool, Preston, Blackburn and Burnley, and others at occasional markets in towns within a seventy-mile striking distance. He drovc a Volvo with an in-car telephone and a horde of gadgets.

He was a born salesman but now concentrated on administration, stock control, collecting the takings and fiddling a healthy percentage with which to keep his wife up to her ears in thick pile carpet and gold lavatory fittings. Since the break-up of Toni's second marriage he had been exhorting her to stop fooling around and settle down with a 'proper chap'.

Ruth had remained Toni's closest friend. She laughed at the luxury and put plastic covers on the furniture as a joke. She drove a sports car and got heavily drunk with the girls at least once a week.

She stayed well clear of the market stalls but occasionally took a job on cosmetic counters in the big stores to relieve the boredom and stock up on creams, lotions and make-up. Ruth was mad and larger than life.

The couple had no children and visited Toni in America at least once a year. They came to the house the first evening she was back. When she began telling them what Mario had said about the Dysons, she was confident they would say there had been a mistake. That this sort of thing didn't happen in Blackpool.

But they didn't. These things did happen since Steven and Eric Dyson had been in town.

Stuart told her about Leo Sedgwick and Arnold Bateman, the burnt out Roller and the broken arms of the bingo hall bouncers.

"The local tearaways soon got the message. Tearaways like stacked odds. These were stacked against. Arnold couldn't buy protection."

The shock was profound. It was followed by outrage. Mario had been telling the truth. He had been deliberately run down, his body mangled, in an attempt to make him sell.

The Rossettis had worked for three generations for what they had. The Dysons wanted it a lot quicker and were prepared to use broken limbs and blackmail to get it.

"I'm not going to let it happen to Mario. I know this town. Better than the Dysons ever will. And the family still has influence and friends here. I'm going to fight them."

Stuart looked grim.

"Toni. The family always had influence but it was never the Mafia. If you tell people about the Dysons they won't believe you. They won't want to believe you. When I heard the rumours, I didn't. The Dysons are respectable, they're clever and they have all the right contacts in all the right places.

"They also have a small army. Okay, anyone can hire seasonal woodentops as bouncers. No brains but a dinner jacket. But they have pros from Manchester and two very nasty characters in charge.

"And where are you going to find your friends? Carleton Cemetery? The old crowd from your father's and grandfather's days are gone. What have you got left, apart from us?"

The names went through her mind. In-laws, cousins, contacts from the old days. Marcello Nicolato and Anthony Maselli, both dead, their children anglicised and spending their inheritance out of town. The hardman Luciano Pisani, retired to Naples with a wife thirty years his junior; Abe Goldman of hamburger fame, asthmatic in St Annes. Uncle Vittorio dead, Uncle Emilio on the run in Malta.

"So what do I do, Stuart?"

"God knows. Negotiate? Maybe this time they'll settle for a genuine partnership."

But that wasn't good enough. They had hurt Mario and she wanted to hurt them back. Selling out or accepting them as partners was out of the question. She had to talk to them face to face, had to see with whom she was dealing. Reputation was a false yardstick by which to measure anyone. She had to judge them for herself.

They had been eager to meet her. She had gone the next day, armed with Mario's authority to offer up to £100,000 for the return of the shares.

The frontage of The Life of Riley was painted green. The name was picked out in five-foot-high pink letters at first-floor level. The taxi took her round the corner and stopped alongside the rear extension, a plain white-stuccoed two-storey building. She was met by Steven

Dyson, who pressed her hand with more intimacy than necessary for a formal greeting.

He was elegant, in an Austin Reed suit, and had an undefined air that fascinated as well as caused her disquiet. His brother was waiting, he said, in an upstairs conference room. He indicated a flight of stairs and she suspected his manners. A real gentleman would have led the way; he wanted to catch her rear view.

The conference room was a thirty-foot by fifteen-foot lounge, decorated and furnished with Habitat taste, with a bar in one corner. Very suburban Cheshire.

Eric Dyson was a large avuncular man with a premature bald head and shiny pink cheeks. Toni knew he was late thirties but he could have passed for middle fifties. He would have looked good at a Greyfriars' reunion.

These were Mario's hit men?

Steven had poise. No affectations and little jewellery. A black signet ring and a Rolex. She had met his type before. The two years she had lived in Richmond and the movie parties. Men who were totally self-assured and used to getting what they wanted. The charm oozed and people acquiesced. It was due to a combination of breeding, education and good looks. Steven Dyson had it all, but what gave him an extra edge was that he almost totally hid his condescension. Almost.

It was that percentage of detectable deceit that had given her a moment's disquiet. She became more at ease when she recognised it. The breed might be clever and successful and, in Steven Dyson's case, dangerous, but they all had one common factor. They were little boys who wanted their own way and who got very cross when someone said no.

They exchanged polite small talk about Mario's well-being and Emilio's whereabouts before finally getting down to business. Eric negotiated while Steven spent most of the time looking at her legs. Toni made her top offer and Eric countered with £200,000 for the whole business. She closed the discussion.

"Rossetti Entertainments is not for sale."

"Perhaps Mario should decide," Eric said. "Perhaps he will see things differently. You will be returning to America but he has to live here. Early retirement could be attractive to him. While he still has what's left of his health."

The directness of the threat surprised her. She hadn't thought he would be so obvious.

Downstairs, Steven apologised for his brother. "I'll talk to him. I would hate things to get acrimonious between us." He smiled. "Perhaps I can offer you dinner?"

"Perhaps."

"Tonight?"

"Not tonight." She smiled back and tried to make it warm. She pressed his fingers when they shook hands. "I'll call you."

Eric talked business but Steven played games. She liked games. But that was before she discovered the sort of games he had planned

Chapter 7

THE memory of the car park was one she had tried to block from her mind. But sharing the burden of her problems with Maudie had been like visiting a psychiatrist. She now felt strong enough to face it – and to attempt to exorcise it from her nightmares.

She lay back on the bed in her hotel haven, and remembered every detail.

It happened after she had seen the Dysons. The day had been fraught and a night out with Ruth was a welcome relief. Her friend's bubbling personality lifted the gloom and, once again, made Toni doubt the seriousness of the brothers' threats.

They dined at a country pub grill room before calling at Dolly's for an hour. Toni wanted to make a proprietorial appearance. They chatted with Jimmy Doc until midnight when Ruth suggested a nightcap at a gambling club where the atmosphere was more restrained.

Instead of disco there was the rhythmic click of chips, the murmur of croupiers and the swish of cards on green baize. Two games of chemin de fer were in progress.

"This is the serious room," Ruth said. "Roulette and the amateurs are downstairs."

Toni recognised three or four faces. They were elderly and wealthy. From a Blackpool of another age. They acknowledged her with nods from across the tables and one held her hand paternally for a few moments while he asked about Mario and said she had a look of her father.

"They're the last of their generation," Ruth said, as they nursed vodka and tonics. "I know people keep saying it, but it's true – the town has changed. There's no longer the money here. Oh, the landladies go off to Benidorm every November, but they do it with the rates money these days.

"It used to be that the profits made in Blackpool stayed here. There were lots of men like your father and grandfather. They lived here, made their money here, and spent it here. Not now. The multinationals have moved in and it's become London money. It goes straight down south to the corporation banks.

"Have a walk around town and you'll see the results. It used to be that the dress shops here rivalled London. They weren't for holidaymakers, they were for people like you and me. Rich bitches. Now they're either closing down or changing their stock. Have been for the last ten years. Nobody's spreading the gravy any more. It's all going south. Delfont. First Leisure."

Toni said, "So people like Steve and Eric Dyson are more than welcome?"

"I should say so. Young, pushy. They get things done and they spend. They give everybody hope."

"Not everybody."

"No. Not everybody."

Toni yawned.

"You've lost your stamina," Ruth laughed.

"I've got old."

"Maybe you should settle down. Try marriage again."

"I've tried marriage."

"Third time lucky?"

"There's no such thing as luck. You make your own."

"You're too cynical. You never know. You might meet Mr Right. Fall in love."

"I used to fall in love. Now I just fall in lust."

"Ooh. Bitch."

Toni yawned again.

"Excuse me," she said sheepishly.

Ruth shook her head.

"No stamina. Not even for lust. I remember when . . ."

"Not memory lane. It makes me feel older."

"Okay, Cinderella. I'll take you home."

A dinner-jacketed all-in wrestler unlocked the door to let them out and Ruth made sotto voce comment on the cut of his trousers.

"It looks like a piece of lead piping," she said. "With my luck, that's what it would be."

They both laughed as they crossed the car park.

Ruth's sports car looked out of place among the limousines. So did the Ford van parked alongside it. Maybe that belonged to holidaymakers who had gone downstairs where the noise was louder, the clientele less select, and the odds were legally stacked heavily in favour of the house with roulette, dice and blackjack.

They were almost at the car when the man stepped out from behind the van.

"Jesus Christ!" Ruth said.

Toni looked behind. Two more men had appeared. They were dressed in dark trousers and sweaters. There was nowhere to run.

"You gave us a shock," Ruth said to the one in front.

There was a catch in her voice. The keys rattled in her hand as she attempted to open the car door.

"Not so fast," the man said, and moved to stand in front of the door. His accent was soft and Irish. "We've only just met."

The fear hit Toni's stomach. It was a whisk that threatened to get out of control. She took a deep breath to try to ease the paralysis in her arms and legs, and turned to look at the other two. One leaned on the rear of the van, the other stepped closer. Both were grinning with the power of the situation.

"Don't scream," the nearest one said conversationally. He held up a Stanley knife so that she could see it clearly.

"It wouldn't be worth it. I could open your face so quick you wouldn't feel it."

She knew it. He didn't have to say it. Perhaps he wanted to say it. She stared at his face, trying to memorise it, pretending she would be able to do something about it afterwards.

"What do you want?"

It was such a lame bloody question she wished she hadn't asked it. At this particular moment, they could take anything they damned well pleased.

He moved her with his left hand and she let him, her eyes watching the blade of the Stanley knife and, beyond it, his grinning face. He moved her until she was between him and the man at the rear of the van. She could sense him close behind her.

"Well, you are a beauty, aren't you?" he said. He held the knife inches from her face and stroked her cheek with the fingers of his left hand. "A real classy piece of cunt."

The word was a smack in the face. It was crude and horrible and it was being used as a weapon, like the knife, to frighten and belittle her.

"Get on with it," she said. The word had angered her. "You haven't got long. Other people will be leaving the club any minute. I saw them getting ready." She plucked two names from the past. "Peter Isaacs and Mike Bennett. They'll be out any second . . ."

"Shut up."

The knife rested against her nose. She told herself he was not going to use it. Whatever they were going to do, they were not going to cut her. The knife was a threat to make her obey. She would obey, for now. She shut up.

She felt hands on her buttocks. The one behind was feeling her body.

"This is a dangerous town," said the man with the knife. His left hand dropped to her breasts. "A very dangerous town for a woman on her own."

Her skirt was being raised. She felt sick, not with fear

but revulsion. His accent. What was his accent? Think of other things to divert attention from the hands above her stockings.

The accent was flat and northern but the regional edge had been smoothed away. It was an anonymous accent. His face? Although she had stared at it initially, it had failed to make an impression. The knife had dominated her senses. She looked past the blade so that the sharp edge blurred out of focus.

He was late twenties, square face, no distinguishing marks, thin fair hair, cut short, wisped over his forehead. His grin showed his teeth. They were surprisingly white and even, not false. His smile was designed to display them.

"You know, you need protection if you plan on staying around here," he said.

She shuddered and tried to ignore the hands. She couldn't maintain her control much longer. It would end in a scream of rage or a wild swing at the grinning face. She breathed deeply again and concentrated on the scent of the sea.

The waves sounded muted from beyond the casino and across the deserted promenade. The only other sound was the occasional purr of a passing car, probably a taxi, taking nightclubbers home to a safe bed.

"Just think what we could do. If we wanted," he said.

His left hand squeezed her breast and twisted it, so that she gasped at the pain.

A car turned off the promenade and drove down the road alongside the casino. It didn't stop but its engine noise stopped him hurting her. His expression changed and he looked over her shoulder at the man behind her, his eyes giving orders.

The hands were removed and her skirt fell back into place. She heard footsteps crossing the gravel of the car park. Relief waited to flood in.

Was that it? Was it over?

"You should be more careful in future." The grin had returned and he made patterns with the knife before her face. "Next time we could get serious."

A car engine started somewhere close and he stepped past her and went round the back of the van. She slumped against its panelled side, her eyes closed, her body trembling. Car doors slammed. The car drove away.

"God," Ruth said. "Are you all right?"

Toni gulped for saliva.

"I'm all right."

She opened her eyes and saw Ruth sitting against the bonnet of the car, clutching her handbag.

"Did they . . . hurt you?" Ruth asked. Her voice was shaky.

"No. They didn't hurt me. You?"

"He asked for a kiss!" Ruth laughed nervously. "He was such a big bugger."

"What did you do?"

"What did I do? I fucking kissed him."

Neither of them laughed.

Toni felt no relief. There was no room for it. She was too full of anger.

The assault had been planned to demonstrate how vulnerable she was, and to frighten her. What had annoyed her was that it had succeeded so well.

There had been no point going to the police. Technically the men had been guilty of threatening behaviour and indecent assault but it was the sort of situation that occurred many times each night in the season and that was rarely reported to the law.

Neither she nor Ruth had been physically hurt, nothing had been stolen and the men would be impossible to trace in a town seething with strangers. If they were found, it would be difficult to prove anything.

If she had been a man the assault would have been violent, but it was no consolation that she had not been hurt. If she had been a man she could have fought back and she would not have had to suffer the indignities of strange hands being intimate with her body.

The assault had not deterred her. Like the attack on Mario, it had made her all the more determined to fight back. She wanted the grinning ape with the Stanley knife hurt and, if necessary, was prepared to do the hurting.

After three days, the anger still came in waves, like jetlag. She was adjusting to the time difference between two continents but she couldn't adjust to the humiliation she had suffered.

She had told Ruth that she wanted to hit back.

"But how?" her friend had asked. "They're bastards."

Her reply had been cold and simple.

"By being bigger bastards."

It was time to meet Maudie and hope he had found her some.

Chapter 8

MAUDIE had been nervous while waiting in the shop for her to return. He couldn't be sure if he looked halfway presentable or simply a pathetic echo of his past. Jack the lad with a bus pass and an invite to all the senior-citizen bun fights.

Compared to how she had first seen him that afternoon, the suit and shirt were a definite improvement. But then, an undertaker's body bag would have been an improvement.

The Mercedes pulled up outside and he walked towards it, as self-conscious as a first date.

Toni looked twice and then again. The trouble had been worthwhile.

"That's some transformation," she said.

"It had to be. For both our sakes." He directed her to drive towards Bow. "It's a tandoori house. The food's good, the place is clean and at this time of night there'll be no drunks sleeping in the pappadums. Where are you staying?"

"One of London's faceless hotels. Indifferent service and high rates. America has spoiled me. I think bad manners must be a British tourist attraction."

She wore tailored trousers and a cashmere sweater, both black, and a lot of gold. She looked good and made him feel good. He was in a limousine with a beautiful woman. It was as if he were reliving the high times of thirty years before.

They were the only customers at the New Delhi

Tandoori Restaurant but the barber who had recommended it was right. It was clean and the food was excellent. When they had eaten and coffee had been served, he began.

"Toni, what you were talking about this afternoon. You were talking about a war. I don't know anybody big enough to have a quiet word with the Dysons, to warn them off. So, if you don't sell out, you're left with a war. That's nasty. Is that what you want?"

"I don't want it, but if there's no other way, then that's what I'll settle for."

He mulled over his next question before asking it.

"Why? I mean, women usually run a mile from violence. They don't like it. You feel loyalty to Mario. But a war? It's not ladylike."

"Don't get confused about me being a woman, Maudie. I know all about roles and how I should behave. I learned it at an early age. I was the first born and my father wanted a son. I loved him very much and he loved me but I grew up feeling guilty I wasn't a boy."

She lit a cigarette and he waited for her to continue.

"The world, his world, revolved around men. He was father and godfather. Women were there to bear children and wear black. Then he died. What did I do? I went looking for a substitute. I got two beauties.

"They were okay, in their way, but I learned that role-playing didn't make a man any stronger than a woman. Physically, they were stronger. But not in any other way.

"I've known a lot of men since. None seriously. None have made me want to know them seriously. Most men are defective when you get past their image. Their emotions and perceptions are two-dimensional. They can be pretty poor substitutes for women. So forget ladylike. I'm a person and I'm not going to be pushed around."

"That's quite a speech," said Maudie.

She laughed.

"I'm sorry if I sound bitter. Usually I try not to let it

show. I'm not a feminist. I like the attention I get from men. But the roles I play, I now play for me. I got fed up of being used by men a long time ago. All they ever gave me were bruises, inside and out. Well, not the Dysons. Not this time. This time, I'm going to do the screwing."

He drank some coffee and pushed his cup and saucer around on the starched table cloth with one finger. He stopped pushing, lay the hand flat on the table and tapped softly with his fingertips.

"You don't know a lot about me, Toni."

"What I know, I like. Isn't that enough?"

He smiled.

"It's a nice thing to say but it's not practical. Not for a hard-headed business woman." He raised his eyebrows. "Business person. I want to tell you about me."

"All right."

"Eighteen years ago you were a girl. Impressionable. You were good for my ego. I think that probably you got a wrong impression. I was never a white knight. I was always a villain.

"I meant what I said about your grandfather. He was a likable man. And about Jack Spot. There were loyalties in those days, but that was in the forties and fifties. Let me start at the beginning."

He told her about his upbringing, his graduation in crime from Borstal to military prison to jail. About his association with the London gangs, and working for the Krays. He told her enough for her to understand, without detailing the full extent of what he had done.

"Five years with The Firm. Not a peaceful time. But once you were in, it was hard to get out. Ronnie finally went round the bend and I was bloody relieved when they were put away. He had a death list a mile long. It's a pound to a penny I was on it."

The coffee had gone cold. He waved to a waiter and ordered another plus a brandy. Toni declined.

"After that, I was involved in capers that went wrong.

They were violent. I shot a security guard. He was doing his job, I was doing mine. I was a limit boy. That means that once I started I would go the limit. No matter what it took. I've damaged a lot of people. Most of them deserved it. I've seen people killed. I am not nice to know."

She lit a second cigarette from the first. Her face was pale and serious.

"Why the confession, Maudie?"

He drank the brandy and sipped the coffee.

"When I came out of prison the last time, the only thing I wanted was never to go back. I could think of nothing worse. But there is something worse. Sitting in a deckchair in a second-hand shop, reading paperback books is worse. It's like being dead. That's all I'm doing there. Waiting for death."

He drank the rest of the brandy.

"I don't want to wait any more. You've put me back in a suit and a clean shirt and I like it. I was excited this afternoon at the thought of seeing you tonight. I haven't been excited in eight years. Jesus Christ, my biggest thrill is finding books I haven't read among the junk Tommy buys. Now hear me out before you turn me down, but I want to go north with you.

"I can do a job for you, I know I can. I'm sixty-three. Sixty-four in September. But I've got that feeling in my gut again that makes me want to go the limit. I can't do anything else. I do my trade or I become a drunk. I've had a bellyful of being down and I want to work again. I want the excitement again. I want life again."

Toni said nothing. She continued to watch him through the smoke of her cigarette.

"This job is important to me," he said. "Because you came looking for help and because it's my last chance. I won't let you down, Toni, because if I do, I'll be letting myself down.

"I've worked with the best. Or the worst. Depends how

you look at it. I understand mobs and violence and protection. I've done security and I've been an enforcer. The Dysons are playing at it. A couple of Archies. I can take them. Any way you want me to. Will you let me?"

She stubbed out the cigarette and called to a waiter for the bill.

"I'm paying," she said. "I told you. It's business."

The waiter took the money away and they stared at each other.

She said, "How does ten thousand pounds sound? Plus expenses?"

He felt the prickle at the back of his eyes and blinked to control it. It would be a hell of a thing for a limit boy to cry with joy. He held his hand across the table and she took it. They shook.

"Toni, I'd do it for free."

They left the restaurant and got back in the car.

"How about a drink now?" she said.

"I was hoping you'd say that, gel. There's a couple of boozers I'd love to be seen in, with you. Do my pride the world of good."

"There's nothing wrong with your pride, Maudie."

He grinned. He was a pools winner who'd just had a heart transplant. There was nothing he couldn't do, and putting a look of amazement on some East End faces was one of them.

"Before we go for a drink, there's more business to discuss. I'll need some cash up front. For . . . equipment."

"Equipment?"

They exchanged a look. She was the guvnor. She had a right to know.

"Shooters."

She nodded. She accepted the need.

"How much?"

"I don't know exactly, but it'll cost. I saw a man earlier

and told him what I wanted. It depends what he can get. A grand, maybe more."

She reached for her handbag, which was on the back seat of the car, and opened it. From an inner zippered compartment she took two packets of notes that were still in their bank wrappers. She hesitated for an instant before handing them over. Perhaps this was the real moment of decision.

"Two thousand. Expenses. You keep an account, Maudie, and tell me when you need more."

Two grand in fifties. It felt like hardly anything at all but it had been an act of faith for her to hand it over. He wanted to tell her that he wouldn't abuse her faith, that the money would be spent correctly.

"The bloke I'm seeing. He's called the Chinaman. I said I'd phone him, if it's on, and see him at one o'clock. You can come if you want. See what you're buying." He was putting it clumsily, damaging their trust by putting it into words. "I mean, it might be interesting for you. A visit to the underworld."

"No thanks, Maudie. You're the professional. You sort it out. But one thing. Buy me a gun, too. In case."

He was shocked at the request. Guns were serious. People who used them had to accept the risks involved. He didn't want Toni to carry.

"Would you use it?"

Her face was serious.

"If necessary."

"If it meant killing someone?"

She hesitated. Then nodded.

"I think so."

At this moment she meant it. Whether she would be able to pull the trigger if the circumstances arose, was something else.

"What did they do, Toni?"

"Don't you think they've done enough?"

He nodded.

"Perhaps. But is there something you haven't told me?"

She stared ahead, as if remembering, then took a cigarette from her bag and depressed the dashboard lighter.

"I've told you everything else, but this is personal. It makes no difference to how we fight the Dysons. It makes no difference to our deal. It's just something that helped me make up my mind as to how far I was prepared to go."

She lit the cigarette.

Maudie nodded. Perhaps he would be able to talk her out of it later.

"Now," she said, and grinned to lighten the mood. "Let's go for that drink. Show me the East End."

He laughed.

"With pleasure, gel. The full ten-bob tour. But mind the falling bodies. People round here don't believe in miracles. Lazarus in a new whistle and with a stunner on his arm could cause a few coronaries. At least, I bleeding hope so."

Chapter 9

MAUDIE travelled north by train from Euston wearing his second-hand suit and carrying a hold-all and a Samsonite suitcase.

The hold-all contained new clothes that included shirts, slacks, a sweater and windcheater jacket. The reinforced and rigid suitcase contained his purchases from the Chinaman.

He had done very well and had listened more carefully to the advice of the arms broker than he had years before when he thought he knew everything. Times and weapons change and he had been guided by the Chinaman.

He travelled first class to be able to watch his luggage more easily and read the Elmore Leonard during the journey. He was enjoying himself. His attitude was ten years younger already. Action had always been exciting, now it was rejuvenating.

So far, he hadn't attempted to plan any aspect of the job. It was in Blackpool so he let it stay there. The time to start thinking about it was when he arrived, when he saw the fighting ground and could assess the opposition. Anway, he was still a hired hand. He would be operating under the direction of Toni, although on his own terms.

At the moment he had the advantage because anything that was going to happen was going to be caused by him. He was a secret guided weapon, targeted courtesy of British Rail.

It was all a bit like a *Boy's Own* adventure and that was

another aspect that pleased him. He had always enjoyed adventure, even growing up in Bow and Bethnal Green. Home had been an airey, a basement flat, in a high Victorian terrace opposite the Dragon pub. Mean streets but a great community spirit, and there was always Vicky Park nearby to provide a feel of the country.

He never remembered his father, who had done a bunk while Maudie was still a baby, but he had never felt deprived. His gran and mum had made sure of that.

His gran – he could see her now – supervising the oven and steaming pans each Sunday dinner time, while pouring Guinness from the jug he had brought from the Dragon across the road.

He hadn't thought about it for years but the smell was there, hot and appetising in his memory.

His mum, well, she'd been a bit of a gel, but who could blame her?

Looking back, you only saw the good things, but there had been plenty of hard times, too. It had been inevitable that he would turn out the way he had.

Even the war hadn't straightened him out. He had gone from juvenile crime to call-up to dishonourable discharge, once the hostilities had ceased, for redistributing army supplies on the black market.

It had all been essential experience and a necessary part of his criminal education. There had been nothing else for him but to be a villain.

In his younger days he had fully accepted that his acts of violence and dishonesty were unlawful and unjustifiable in the eyes of society. But that was all right because he had never considered himself to be part of society.

He had strong views, though, that it was necessary to have rules and standards for people to live by. If you didn't, people like him wouldn't have been able to make a living.

But society's standards had always been faulty. You only had to look at how the rich got richer and the poor got shat on. You could even blame the faults of the system for his life of crime. At least, a good brief could make a case of it.

Maudie laughed at himself silently. Old age was turning his brain soft. The reason he had become a villain was because he had gained a reputation for violence in his youth. He had liked both the reputation and the excitement of violence. It had brought instant friendships, camaraderie and ego. The power had been a drug and he had become professional, his violence clinical and divorced from feeling.

His professionalism had brought rewards and punishments, and the last punishment had finally chipped loose his certainty. For the first time he had assessed his past and discovered emptiness.

But, as in the song, he could allow no regrets. It was his past. It was the only thing he owned. He hadn't dared look into the future.

Now he had a new lease on life. Nothing long term. Christ, at his age nothing could be long term. But there was something to look forward to, danger to anticipate, violence to face. Most of all, a justification.

It was nice, just for once, to be on the side of the angels.

He took a taxi from the station to the address Toni had given him that morning on the telephone. It was about a mile inland, along a main artery littered with traffic lights and parades of shops, and signs on lamp posts that pointed to the park, the zoo, the model village.

They turned off into a street of red-brick terraced houses. The front doors of some opened directly on to the street, others had small gardens, although many of the gardens had been demolished and paved to make car parking spaces. The houses were two- and three-storey and many had loft extensions.

Number 24 was a two-storey end-terrace, a third of the

way along. Its garden was intact and there was a narrow lane a car-width wide that ran alongside to the next street.

He rang the bell and the door was opened by a vivid, black-haired young woman. Her look was an appraisement.

"You must be Maudie."

"You must be Ruth."

She opened the door wider to let him enter.

"Go through."

He went along the passage and into a small dining room at the rear. A kitchenette led off like a finger that pointed down a long thin back garden.

"I'm making tea. Unless you'd like something stronger?"

"Tea will be lovely."

He put the bag and the suitcase in a corner and sat in an easy chair where he could look into the kitchenette and watch Ruth making tea. They exchanged looks. His blank but friendly, hers suspicious.

"Toni will be here soon. Milk and sugar?"

"Yes please. Two sugars."

She brought the tea in a red mug. Hers was in a green mug.

"Is this your house?"

"No. It belongs to a friend. A girl I know. Toni rented it from her." She smiled tentatively. "An offer she couldn't refuse."

"Toni can be a persuasive girl."

Ruth stared while sipping the tea.

"We've met before, you know. Years ago. The last time you were up here."

He shrugged.

"It was a long time ago. I'm afraid I don't remember."

"No reason you should. I was young and silly and we only actually met the once. Toni wanted to keep you for herself. Everyone was a bit frightened of you."

He smiled.

"I hope they still will be."

Her mouth dropped slightly open and then she laughed. "Yes. I see what you mean." Her expression became more serious. "I think they should be."

He felt good to be taken seriously, even by a young woman whose judgment might be faulty. It helped his confidence.

The doorbell rang and Ruth jumped. He was pleased that he showed no reaction.

"That'll be Toni," she said, and went to let her in.

He stood and stretched to ease the stiffness and waited, as if for inspection, at the far side of the room. At ease, feet apart, hands held across his groin.

She came along the passage quickly and stopped in the doorway. She gave him a swift once-over, re-assessing what she had hired. Then she smiled warmly and relaxed.

"Hi, Maudie. Any trouble?"

"No trouble."

He wondered if she had been worried in case he didn't turn up. Or, worse, turned up and found to be unsuitable in the cold light of reason.

"Do you want a cup of tea?" Ruth asked. "I've just made some."

"Yes. Please."

Toni sat down and the tension went. Maudie picked up his tea and took a hardback seat by the window that looked into the back garden.

"Nice house," he said.

"It's quiet and anonymous. It's one of the few private ones left in the street. All the ones with parking areas are flats. Holiday or permanent flats. Either way, the people in them aren't curious. You've got the house to yourself. It's stocked with food. All mod cons. There's beer and whisky and stuff in the cabinet in the front room. Help yourself."

Ruth came back with the tea. Toni's was in a yellow

mug. He wondered if the colours were significant. They all sat and sipped. A Technicolor tea party.

"How much does Ruth know?" he asked.

"She knows the situation. She knows you've come to help."

"Does she know how?"

"If it comes to that, yes."

He looked at Ruth.

"You know my name, that I'm from London and that I'm a villain."

"I won't tell anybody, if that's what you mean."

"That's what I mean."

She became red with anger.

"Toni. Tell him I'm safe. I won't talk."

"Ruth is my closest friend, Maudie. You can trust her. I trust her totally."

"Coppers can get very cross if you mess up their manor."

"I won't talk. I've been questioned by police before."

He raised his eyebrows in a question.

"Drugs," Toni said. "Pills and pot. The Swinging Sixties?"

He smiled.

"You've got form?"

"No. The first time we were released the next day. The second time we had to make statements at the station. We were hanging out with a rock band that kept getting busted. The police bit was heavy at the time. It happened at an impressionable age."

"They put you off drugs?"

"No. I grew up. Vodka is a lot less complicated if you want oblivion."

He laughed.

"Ruth. Are you married?"

"Yes."

"What about your husband?"

"He's not involved."

"But you are?"

Toni said, "He knows you're here. That I've brought someone in to help with security. He thinks I'm still negotiating with the Dysons."

"Is he a friend?"

"A very close friend."

"But he wouldn't approve if he knew the full story?"

"No."

"Wise man."

He laughed again.

"All right. But if this gets messy, two things: I want both of you out of it, totally. And if the law does get stroppy and you are whisked away to the nick, remember the golden rule: stay shtum until you get a brief. Even then you don't know nothing."

They nodded and he drank his tea.

"Nice tea," he said to Ruth. She smiled.

"Did you get what you needed in London?" Toni asked.

He nodded but made no move to open the suitcase. That was his business, not theirs. It would only make them nervous.

"Have you had a change of mind?" he asked Toni.

"No. But I think we might be able to short circuit the problem."

"How?"

"By getting back Emilio's books and the papers he signed. I know where they are."

He raised an eyebrow.

"I had dinner with Steven Dyson. It was a business dinner. He pretended to increase their offer and I pretended to accept it. But I insisted on seeing the books before anything was finalised, to prove they really had them. He took me to The Life of Riley. They're in a steel filing cabinet, behind the bar in the upstairs conference room."

"So you're suggesting burglary?"

"More like armed persuasion. It would be a one-to-one situation, late at night. Two to one, counting me. We would have to persuade Steven Dyson to unlock the cabinet. It wouldn't be difficult. The key is on his key ring."

"That would be armed robbery. You start pretty close to the top, don't you? He could call the police."

"I don't think so. What we're stealing is evidence of blackmail as well as sharp business practice."

He thought about it. The books were a stumbling block to any sort of solution.

"It wouldn't end it," he said. "The Dysons wouldn't let it go at that. They can't be seen to be beaten. They'd come after you. If they can't have the business they'll wreck it. Making Steven Dyson look a burk will be a declaration of war."

"Wrong, Maudie. War was declared the night they drove over Mario's legs."

Chapter 10

RUTH drove Maudie round the resort in a hire car so that he could get a sense of the pace and the size of the town.

Toni had supplied him with two street maps. One was pinned on a bedroom wall at the house, the other lay open on his lap and he followed their progress across the folds with a finger. Their route went past the properties of both the Dysons and the Rossettis.

Maudie had given Toni explicit instructions in London two days before, and the speed with which they were being carried out was hard to believe.

He was in command, in action, butterflies at six o'clock and feeling better than he had in years. It was only now that he was becoming fully aware how far his life had slumped.

Booze had veiled the truth to an extent. Not that it had been a serious problem. He hadn't had enough money in recent years for it to become a serious problem. But he had used booze to provide highs and lows in the perpetual plane of his deckchair existence.

When he was working he had always kept booze under strict control. There were a lot of blokes he had known who hadn't been able to operate without a skinful, but not Maudie. It was unprofessional.

They were driving slowly along the front from south to north. The North Pier was on the left, a busy square on the right. Trams rumbled and crowds herded at crossing points in the bright afternoon sunshine.

"Can you stop along here?" he said.

"If there's somewhere to park."

Ruth drove on, past the Metropole Hotel, turned right across the traffic into a side street and began to cruise in search of a parking place. She couldn't find one.

"Let me out and pick me up in fifteen minutes. I just want to stretch my legs."

"Okay."

He got out and watched the car drive away. It was hotter than he had thought. He should have changed out of the suit into something lighter.

The street was quiet. He was standing outside what looked like a chapel. He turned and walked back towards the sea.

The trams were fascinating and, at this stretch of the Promenade, their tracks swerved around the bulk of the Metropole and into the road itself, so that they mingled with ordinary traffic. They clanged warnings to cars to make way.

He crossed, skirted the concrete sculptures of a crazy golf course, and stood by the railings of the sea wall and looked at the horizon. Its vastness surprised him. He had forgotten such expanses existed. His own horizons had been so small for so long.

The sun glinted off the sea and hurt his eyes. He turned his back on it and watched the people pass by. This end of town was more sedate and the people were mainly elderly. He didn't look out of place.

Perhaps he could pick up a well-off widow before he had finished. The thought was meant as a joke but it lingered as a consideration. He could do worse.

He walked back, stretching his shoulders and trying to ease the recurring stiffness in his leg.

There was a tobacconist on the corner and he went in. It was cool and shady and the aroma of tobacco was pleasant. In the old days, when the money was easy, he had smoked cigars. He bought a packet of stubby half coronas and a box of matches and on his way out noticed a display of sunglasses. He bought a pair that adjusted to the light so that they could be worn indoors.

Back in the street, he felt self-conscious. He couldn't make up his mind whether he was playing at nostaligia, virility or being a holidaymaker.

Ruth pulled up alongside him and got in the car.

"Nice glasses," she said, and continued the tour.

After another hour he allowed Ruth to drop him off back at the house, declining her offer to cook him a meal.

He familiarised himself with the layout of the property, working out escape routes if they became necessary, and enjoying the novelty of having a modern house, if only on a temporary basis.

The front room was small but luxurious compared with what he was used to. Fitted carpets, a deep armchair and a sofa, TV and video, a cassette hi-fi system and racked tapes, flowers in vases. A woman's touch.

He bent to sniff the flowers and discovered they were plastic. A working woman's touch.

In the kitchen, the larder and refrigerator were well stocked. So far, it was a five-star holiday.

Toni came at seven thirty and he went into the kitchen to make a pot of tea. She watched from the dining room.

It was role reversal from that afternoon. He was settled in and domesticated already, acting like a householder, being hospitable, making tea over which to discuss armed robbery and worse.

It was a crazy world.

"We need to talk, Toni. About this whole thing."

"Are you having second thoughts?"

He paused between putting tea bags into the pot to stare at her.

"I'll do a job for you, gel. Don't doubt it. But I want you to be sure you want me to."

She walked into the front room. When she returned a few minutes later she was smoking a cigarette.

"I've thought about it a lot. I'm not doing this on a whim. There are two courses I can take. Accept their offer and persuade Mario to sell out. Or fight back.

"Selling out means handing over a three-generation business for peanuts. It means Emilio will spend his retirement years in shame. It means Mario will be exiled to suntan his crippled legs abroad. It means they will both be unavenged, and a pair of arrogant shits will go on to do the same thing to some other poor sod.

"I left this town by choice but I might want to come back some day. My brother doesn't want to go at all."

He poured boiling water into the pot.

She said, "There isn't any choice. I've got to have a go."

Her stance was defiant and determined. But she still didn't know what she was getting into. He had a duty to tell her before it started. It might be better if she sold out. He was one elderly out of condition man against an organisation.

Whose welfare was he thinking of?

He poured the tea, his in the red mug, hers in the yellow, as before, and handed it to her. They went back into the front room and he lit one of the cigars he had bought that afternoon.

"I used to smoke cigars all the time." He coughed. "My lungs were younger then."

"Say what you've got to say, Maudie. Try to talk me out of it."

"It's not that. It's just that you've never seen violence. You don't know what it's like."

"I didn't start the violence."

He decided he didn't like the cigar and put it in an ashtray. Perhaps he should stick to Bombay bits.

"The Dysons," he said. "They're pretend Krays. They've built what they've got the same way. An acceptable front and strong-arm persuasion to make the partnerships, take over businesses. At the moment they're small time. They're not hardmen. They employ hardmen. But they have a very mean streak and they're clever.

"If they're to stay successful, they have to stay respectable to all the nice establishment people. Councillors, chamber of trade, Rotary, police. But, out of sight, where it counts, they have to be known as evil swines.

"Getting the books back won't stop them. They can't back down now. Word would get out. The next bloke they decided to lean on might tell them to piss off. So they'll have to make an example of you, Mario, the business. A fire, gas explosion, rape, a face full of stitches. Think of the worst thing that could happen and they might do it."

He sipped his tea and gave her imagination time to develop the theme.

"Do you still want to go ahead with it?" he said.

"Do you have a gun for me?"

He hesitated.

"Yes. But that's no guarantee."

She nodded.

"I want to go ahead. There's no other way."

He picked up the cigar that had now gone out, considered it and put it back in the ashtray. The time for self-delusion was past.

"I'll get the gun."

He went to the bedroom, took the Samsonite suitcase from the top of the wardrobe, and from it took a 9mm Mauser automatic pistol in a chamois cloth. It had a short, finger-length barrel. It was neat enough for a handbag, potent enough to be a stopper at short range.

She had lit another cigarette by the time he got back, and looked more nervous than he had ever seen her.

"Have you ever handled a gun before?"

"In America. We were out in the woods, fooling around. One of the guys had a revolver. I fired it a couple of times. I didn't like it."

"Did you hit anything?"

"A tree. It was not the tree I was aiming at."

He held out the Mauser for her to see.

"It's automatic. Easy to use. And it kills. Remember that if you point at someone. It's not a toy, to fool around with. It's a deadly weapon. If you use it and you hit someone in the head or chest, chances are you'll kill them. Arms and legs are better targets. But if it comes to using it, I don't suppose there'll be time to make a choice.

"Are you sure you want it?"

Toni took a deep breath and recovered her composure.

"I want it."

"Okay."

He showed her how to load the magazine, where the safety catch was and how to cock the gun.

"It's safe enough, loaded, in your handbag, as long as it's not cocked and it has the safety on. And don't forget. Having it is unlawful possession. Using it is a whole lot more. Try to keep it clean of fingerprints. Handle it with a cloth or wear gloves."

He smiled.

"Of course, that's all good advice if you're planning a job. But if you ever have to use it, chances are there won't be time."

He went through the procedures again and watched while she did the same.

"Remember. It kills. Even if you pull the trigger by accident. So treat it with respect." He got up. "More tea?"

"I think I'd rather have a vodka."

She looked up, the gun held in her palm.

"Have tea. I'll put a couple of sugars in it. It's better for the nerves."

He topped up the mugs and settled into the armchair.

"One other thing. Tell Ruth to stay away from both of us. It might even be better if she went away. A holiday or something."

"Ruth? Why? She's got nothing to do with this."

"She's your friend. If they find out she's helping, or is close to you, she could become a target. If they can't get you, they'll get someone you care about. Or they'll hit the club or the halls. You'd better warn your managers to be careful."

He paused.

"If they hit, then I hit back. Harder."

"Is there no way we can avoid all . . ." she shook her head in her search for words " . . . all that might happen?"

"There is one chance. When we get the books back. If I can convince Steven Dyson that I'm trouble shooting for a London firm and that you have major connections, they might bottle out."

Was it wrong to give her hope? They might lose their nerve. After all, this would be their first real opposition.

But the bigger chance was that Dyson would think he was a pensioner on an away-day ego trip, playing cops and robbers. It all depended on how it went.

"Tell me how we're going to get the books back," he said.

Chapter 11

"YOU seem to be miles away."

"What?"

Steven Dyson reached across the restaurant table and put his hand over hers.

"Don't take it so badly. This was meant as a celebration."

She attempted to hide the revulsion she felt at his touch, and laughed.

"I'm sorry. I was wondering where Uncle Emilio was."

"Listen. It's business. That's all. Don't make it into more than it is. There's no need for family drama. Emilio will get in touch and when he does Mario will tell him he's forgiven. Maybe they'll open a new club. In Malta. Or Italy."

"I don't know. Emilio is an old man. Age carries a lot of pride."

"You know, family rows are the worst. A partner or a friend can make a mistake and be forgiven. But family? Somehow it seems to mean more. It shouldn't. A mistake is a mistake, no matter who makes it. Emilio was a little too fond of the horses. I've known people with worse faults. But he'll come back. Don't worry about it. You and Mario are doing the right thing."

She retrieved her hand to light a cigarette. It was hard even to be civil to Steven Dyson. But she had to be much more than that.

Her behaviour at their first dinner date had been designed to encourage his attentions. She had wanted to manipulate him, to discover where the books were kept and to convince him she and her brother were no longer a threat. She had been almost too persuasive.

The books, as she had told Maudie, were kept in the conference room at Riley's. But she had also discovered Steven had an adjoining bedroom. It had taken all her experience to stay out of it. Tonight, he obviously thought his luck would change. It was an expectation she had to encourage.

"I'm sorry, Steven." She smiled. "You're right. Emilio will come back. Perhaps a fresh start will be good for Mario."

"Of course I'm right."

She allowed him to hold her hand again, before excusing herself.

Inside a cubicle in the ladies', she leaned against the wall and opened her handbag. The gun nestled in a side compartment beneath a pair of tan leather dress gloves.

At this moment she could willingly shoot Steven Dyson. His assurance, calculation and dishonesty were offensive, but his presumption was abhorrent.

She closed the handbag, left the cubicle and checked her face in the mirror.

"Come on, silly bitch. Smile."

She eased the tension out of her features and relaxed her mouth. Two pouts at herself and she was able to smile professionally, convincingly. Two drops of Murine and her eyes sparkled again.

Right, she told herself. The show's back on the road.

Three nights ago they had negotiated the sale of Rossetti Entertainments for £250,000, which was still half price. The deal was supposed to go ahead in Mario's hospital room. This dinner date was confirmation to the Dysons that Mario had capitulated.

Toni was flirtatious throughout the meal. She touched Steven's hand frequently, let him catch her looking at him with lustful eyes and smiled approvingly at his innuendos.

My God. What did he really think of her?

Afterwards, he drove towards The Life of Riley.

"Nightcap?" he said.

"Of course."

She stroked his thigh and felt his muscles react. He stroked her leg and began to pull up her skirt. He was very confident. She squirmed, breathed heavily, and dropped her handbag.

"Damn. Things have spilled out."

He stopped fumbling while she bent to pick up the bag and its contents. To maintain his ego and impatience, she rested her hand on his thigh.

They drove past the brightly lit frontage of The Life of Riley. He went down the side street past the two-storey extension at the rear that contained the offices and his apartment, and parked. She delayed him getting out.

"Don't be so impatient. We have all night."

She kissed him on the lips, then opened her door before it could develop.

The street was quiet. The silence roared in her ears. Her nerves were exposed and she felt light enough to fly.

Steven unlocked the street door of the offices, they went in and he locked it behind them. They went upstairs and he unlocked the conference room and, once inside, his impatience boiled over.

He grabbed her from behind, kissing her neck with his open mouth. His hands roamed possessively over her body, his erection pressed into her buttocks.

"Steven!"

She attempted to break away but he only allowed her to turn to face him so that he could kiss her properly. The loathing rose like bile but she fought it back and forced herself to respond. Her pretence at passion assuaged his and he calmed down.

"Steven. Let's take it slowly."

"I don't think I can."

She pulled away.

"How about a drink?"

He was taking off his jacket.

"I don't want a drink. I want you."

"Don't rush things. There's all night. Look, I have a present for you." She opened her handbag, rummaged, and feigned surprise. "Damn. It must have fallen out in the car. I'll go and get it."

"Toni. I want you now."

"It will only take a minute . . ."

She knew she had miscalculated. On the first dinner date she had promised much without giving a great deal, to get inside information. Tonight she had played the temptress again, but too well. If she didn't give in to the inevitable, he would rape her. He would probably think that was what she wanted. Her pulse pounded. The loathing was mixed with other things. Perhaps she did.

He took her in his arms and kissed her forcefully, his tongue digging into her mouth, his hands pulling up her skirt.

She half resisted, attempting to push him away, pulling her mouth free so that his tongue trailed to her neck and ear.

"The bedroom." He started to push her. "I want you in the bedroom. Now."

She was quivering. Her senses building to screaming pitch.

"No." She pushed back. "No."

It was not resistance. It was encouragement. The situation was now beyond her control and she wanted to be taken.

He twisted her arms so that she was forced to walk past the bar, along a short corridor and into the bedroom. His hips were hard against her buttocks and she squirmed against them, fighting and exciting him. He threw her at the bed and she sprawled across it. Her skirt was high, exposing her stockinged legs. The buttons of her silk blouse had opened.

He pulled off his clothes and she lay watching, making no move to cover herself. Their breath came in gasps, rattling hoarsely in their throats. It was animalistic.

Finally, he was naked. In the dim light she could see that his erection visibly throbbed.

"Come on, you bastard," she whispered. "Make me. make me."

He climbed on to the bed and made her. It didn't take long. The lust was too intense to be maintained for long. Ten minutes at the most.

He didn't undress her but pulled her clothes aside. He covered her mouth with his and she raked his back with her nails. The pain made him twist away and he pushed her arms above her head, holding both her wrists in one hand, while he manoeuvred himself with the other.

His entry made her gasp. Still inside her, he held himself above her and stared into her face. His mouth was open and his eyes were vicious. She stared back, equally without feeling. She rotated her hips hard against him.

"Come on then. Make me come."

It was a command. He obeyed.

Chapter 12

SHE had peaked so high that there was a long way to fall. The loathing started immediately afterwards. She stared at the rectangular shadows on the ceiling made by the light spilling in from the corridor, and wallowed in the revulsion.

Beside her, Steven Dyson stirred and touched her shoulder.

"Incredible," he muttered.

She slid off the bed.

"Bathroom," she said.

His bathroom, like his bedroom, had everything. She washed herself and straightened her clothing but avoided the mirror. When she felt she was passable she went to the bar and poured a large vodka and tonic.

It might not be a very meaningful act and it would not solve anything, but what the hell. She drank it in two gulps and pretended she could feel its effect.

She fucked hard and drank hard. Wasn't she a wow.

She poured another vodka and mixed a gin and tonic and carried both glasses into the bedroom.

He rolled on to his back to take the drink from her, making no attempt to hide his nakedness.

"You are incredible, Toni Rossetti."

"It's been said before."

He reached a hand towards her but she pretended not to see it and walked to the foot of the bed, sipping her drink. When there was distance between them, she turned.

"Your present!"
He grinned.
"I thought I'd just had it."
She grinned back.
"Well, let's say it's a reward. For being good."
God. What appalling dialogue. It felt like her brain had seized up in protest at her body.
"It's in the car," she said. "I'll get it. Where are the keys?"
"In my jacket. Left-hand pocket."
The jacket was in the other room. The key ring had two car keys and five other keys. She went back to the door of the bedroom and held them up.
"This place is like Fort Knox. How do I get out?"
"The two keys together. They're for the outside door."
A Yale and a key for a mortice lock were on a separate ring that was linked to the main one.
"I'll only be a minute."
"Lock the door when you come back."
She nodded and left the room. Thankfully, at last, she went back down the stairs.
The mortice lock was stiff and made a noise when she turned it. She unlatched the Yale and pulled open the door, breathing deeply at the night air.
The street was still silent and she took a step half out of the doorway to look both ways. It was five seconds before Maudie emerged from shadows six feet away. He wore dark slacks and windcheater. He moved silently but with a slight limp. Toni told herself it made him look more sinister.
"I'm sorry . . ." she began.
He put a finger over her lips and shook his head. He stepped past her and she closed the door again but didn't lock it. His right hand came out of the windcheater holding a gun. From a pocket he took what looked like a short fat piece of tubing and screwed it on to the barrel.

His hands gleamed oddly and she realised he was wearing surgical gloves.

Toni went cold. Before, it had been talk and fantasy. She had lived out revenge in her mind. Now it was happening.

Maudie was waiting, the gun pointing at the floor, his face expressionless, his eyes blank. The revulsion that had filled her to excess a few moments ago was now overshadowed by fear.

He nodded and she nodded back and he climbed the stairs. She followed and halfway up suddenly realised that Steven Dyson was naked. Maudie would be able to see what had happened.

She flushed and turned the shame to anger. Let him. It had had to be done. Another example of her ruthlessness.

He paused outside the conference room and lifted the gun to point it at the ceiling. He flexed his fingers around the butt and pushed open the door.

The room was empty and he moved straight to the other door, pointing the gun at the bar until he was sure no one was behind it.

It was like a film. Except no film could capture the tension. Her mouth was dry and she saw her glass on top of the bar. She would have loved to have taken a drink but dare not do anything but trail behind the professional. Her professional.

Maudie looked at her and she pointed and mouthed the words: In the bedroom.

He nodded again, pushed open the door and went down the corridor. The bedroom door was open. He stopped and listened, then stepped inside quickly.

"Jesus Christ!"

Steven Dyson lost his composure.

Toni gulped, licked her lips, and followed.

Maudie was standing at the foot of the bed upon which Dyson still lay naked. He held the gun in two hands and pointed it at the younger man's genitals.

"Put the light on, Toni," Maudie said.

She did so and noticed how small and shrivelled Dyson's penis had become. His face registered open-mouthed shock as he stared from one to the other. His hands still held the gin and tonic she had given him.

"Toni. What . . .?"

"Shut up, toerag."

"Who . . .?"

The gun jerked and coughed in Maudie's hands and the mattress quivered as a bullet hit it, between Dyson's open legs.

"Shit!"

He let go of the glass, spilling the drink on to his stomach, and pulled himself back up the bed in a reflex action.

"Don't speak and don't move," Maudie said.

Dyson froze.

"Get the stuff," he said to Toni.

She realised she had frozen, too. It was not the reaction she should be displaying.

The steel filing cabinet was built into the back of the bar. She went through to the other room, fumbling through the keys to find the one she had seen Steven use three nights before. It fitted and she removed the ledgers and documents and carried them back into the bedroom.

There were two ledgers, of real and falsified figures, the last two sets of audited accounts that had been filed with Companies House and a legal transfer – signed by Emilio, witnessed and attested with a wax seal – that assigned his twenty per cent of Rossetti Entertainments Ltd to the Dysons. The seal would have impressed Emilio.

Among the documents was the loan agreement with the default clause that had trapped him, and there was his notebook that contained lists of contacts and explanations of percentages and how the fiddles worked. He had been recklessly methodical.

She took them all and put them into a plastic Marks and

Spencer carrier bag that she took from her handbag.

Also from the handbag she took a folded document.

"This is a receipt," she said. "It acknowledges the full repayment of Emilio's loan agreement with £10,000 interest, and the return of his shares that you were holding as surety. You will sign it. I'll have it witnessed later. I'll put an even bigger seal on it than you had."

Steven Dyson's mouth worked but no sound came out. He looked at Maudie and back to Toni.

"You may now talk," she said.

"This isn't real. You can't do this."

"It's real and I'm doing it. You'll sign."

"I'll say it was under duress. I'll call the police. Jesus Christ, he damn near shot me."

"There's still time, toerag," Maudie said.

"You won't call the police," Toni said. "You obtained the shares using duress and gambling debts. You can't afford the mud sticking."

"This is madness. You'll never . . ."

"Oh yes I will." She placed the document on the bedside table with a pen. "Sign."

He looked at Maudie again, then leaned across and signed above his name.

"It means nothing," he said.

"But I do, toerag," Maudie said. "Remember that. The Rossettis have friends who don't like to see them being pushed around. Especially by toerags. From now on, the Rossettis are a protected species. No harm will come to them or theirs. If it does, I would advise counting your legs on a morning before you try getting out of bed."

Steven was looking more sure of himself, as if he sensed he wouldn't be harmed.

"Who is he?" he asked Toni. "Is this a joke?"

The gun coughed again and the pillow behind Dyson puffed and sighed.

"The firm I work for have no sense of humour. We

don't just hurt people. We bury them. Sometimes we kill them first."

"No joke, Steven. My family has connections." She had grown back into the role. She must remember not to end with come up and see me some time. "From now on, just leave us alone."

She picked up the shopping bag and walked to the door.

"Is that it?" Dyson asked.

"No, not quite," she said. "The money you signed the receipt for. I've withheld it as compensation for Mario's injuries, medical bills, the damage your cowboys did at the club, and my personal expenses."

He shook his head in disbelief.

"But what about . . . this?"

He flexed himself and spread his arms to indicate the bed and what they had done on it.

"Oh yes. 'That'." She put down the shopping bag and rummaged in her handbag. She threw a 50 pence coin on to the bed. "I suppose you deserve something for 'that'." She smiled. "Keep the change."

She picked up the ledgers and walked out. Her heart was beating fast as she went down the stairs. She couldn't work out if it was excitement or triumph.

At the street door she waited until Maudie came a few seconds later, then followed him to the car. She restrained herself from skipping.

Chapter 13

MAUDIE drove the hire car to the terraced safe house and put it in a garage at the rear. Toni had left the Mercedes there earlier, and they switched cars. This time Toni drove.

At the Rossetti house, the front garden was lit by two lamps, one over the front door and the other over the double garage. Maudie got out and unlocked the garage doors, followed the car in and locked them behind him. They went directly into the house from the garage.

"Set it," Maudie said.

Toni walked through to the cloakroom and switched on the burglar alarm system. Maudie remained in the kitchen, exchanging looks with Jane, the white bull terrier. When Toni came back she laughed.

"Dogs are not funny," he said.

"You've been introduced. She knows you're a friend."

"I hope so."

He moved cautiously as she led the way to the study. Jane watched them go past and then trotted along behind.

There was a second bull terrier, a brindle called Paolo, at large in the extensive back garden. The house was big, but with the alarm, the dogs and high walls out back, along with floodlighting if necessary, Maudie felt reasonably safe.

He had cased the house and made the acquaintance of the dogs that afternoon. The house had impressed him. The dogs had impressed him, too, but in a different way.

There was no arguing with dogs. They didn't understand reason or threat and they were impossible to fight. All you could do in a confrontation was kill them. Alsatians and dobermans were frightening, but bull terriers were more vicious. They fought to the finish.

Toni had pointed out where there was a gap in Jane's teeth.

"She got out one day and a taxi hit her. She bit its bumper bar and tried to shake it. Mario had a hell of a job to make her let go. The driver had to switch off his engine so that she thought she'd killed it."

Paolo, in the garden, was quieter. His hobby, Toni said, was chewing house bricks. No joke.

He hoped they would both remember he was on their side if there was a disturbance.

During the journey from Riley's, Maudie had replayed snatches of the action in his mind. He would dwell on it at length later, but for now, bits came back unbidden like a disconnected trailer.

He had been nervous. Not of getting hurt but of cocking it up. But as soon as he had started up the stairs, the adrenaline had begun to flow, the old feeling had returned.

And, for Christ's sake, it had gone well. Bloody well.

Toni had kept her cool admirably. He could tell afterwards, when they were driving away, that she had been full to bursting with the excitement.

He had seen men whoop, punch, swear and scream away some of the pent-up energy after a successful job. But Toni had bottled it, remained in control of herself.

The bedroom scene had been unexpected and was another eye-opener. Seeing Steven Dyson naked had angered him. He hadn't considered Toni in that way, and the fact that she had shared his bed to obtain what she wanted had upset him.

Her morals were not his business and it shouldn't have upset him. Anyway, it hadn't been a question of morals.

What she had done had been necessary. She was a multi-faceted lady, but he wondered just how tough she really was.

"I think we deserve a drink," she said.

"Just one. It's no night to get tiddly."

"Scotch?"

He nodded and she poured a double.

"No more," he said, taking the glass from her.

"How did we do, Maudie?" Her eyes shone. The excess was just below the surface. It made him feel calmer. Reminded him that he was the pro. "Tell me. Was it good? Was it as good as it seemed?"

"It went all right. I think Mr Dyson got the message."

She laughed.

"It was worth it just to see his face. All of it. I didn't realise what it would be like. I was surprised. It was . . . I don't know what it was like. It was like stepping outside yourself and taking charge. And when you shot the bed . . ."

She poured herself a vodka and tonic and stopped talking. He smiled. She had realised she was too voluble, she was allowing too much to spill out. The image had to be protected, but really she would like to let loose and shout her triumph.

"You did all right, gel."

He raised his glass.

"So did you, Maudie. Thank you."

They drank to each other and she walked across, put her arms round him and held him.

"Thank you," she said again.

After a while, he pushed her away gently.

"It went better than we could have expected. But now it's a waiting game. If they hit back, I don't think it'll be here, tonight. But I'm taking no chances."

He kissed her on the forehead.

"Go to bed, gel. I'll make myself a pot of tea and listen to the world service."

She drained the remainder of the vodka.

"You're right. I'll go to bed but I doubt if I'll sleep. We should have organised a party."

At the door she turned back.

"There are tapes by the television if you get fed up of the radio."

"Goodnight, Toni."

"Goodnight, Maudie. Thanks."

It was a quiet night. No one disturbed its peace. He cleaned the .38 Smith and Wesson and wondered whether they had been good or lucky.

Time was, he had never doubted his own abilities. Self-doubt was a killer, made you think twice, hesitate, and give the other bloke time to do you, before you could do him.

But night was a poor time for memories. Without the distractions of daytime, the memories usually came out sad.

He made a pot of tea and put on a video of a Mario Lanza musical – the tape collection seemed to consist solely of Mario Lanza musicals – and drowned the past in colour and sound.

The night went by with more tea, a couple of catnaps and the radio. By dawn, he also considered he had consolidated his friendship with Jane the bull terrier.

He got up and his leg almost gave way. It had been aching, with varying degrees of ferocity, since he had travelled north. He blamed the dampness and the unusual amount of activity he had been engaged in during the last few days. Normally his exercise consisted of getting in and out of a deckchair in the Tout's shop, or walking the thirty yards to the public bar of The Drum.

The twinges eased as he walked slowly around the room, working the limp away before Toni saw it. He would call at a chemist's shop later and get something for it. Fiery Jack or Deep Heat, lotions and sprays with names like blue films. He had noticed the similarity before and had made a joke about it in The Drum.

"It's the closest I get to sex, these days," he had said.

Now, despite the limp, he thought he might be in shape to try something more substantial than memories.

When the job was done, he would find a middle-aged lady who had taken care of herself and give it a whirl. Nothing young and flighty, somebody he could talk to as well as romance.

With his newfound pride and ten grand in his pocket, who knew what might happen?

He washed and shaved in the downstairs shower room and was cooking bacon and eggs when Toni came into the kitchen. She was wearing jeans and a silk blouse and looked ready to take on the world.

"Smells good," she said.

"I'll do you some."

"No thanks. Much as I'd like. I'll stick to grapefruit and muesli."

"Are you on a diet?"

"No. I eat healthy."

He nodded, and put another slice of bread in the frying pan.

"It works. You look healthy enough for both of us."

They ate together in the kitchen, reading the morning papers while Radio Two provided the perfect domesticated backdrop.

"What do we do today?" she asked.

"Normal business. Only I go with you. High profile. Let them see us and make up their minds. If they're going to reply, it'll be today or tomorrow. It's a small town. They can't leave it too long. Give it a week and start breathing easier. Two, and I can go home."

Home? The bedsit above the shop in Brick Lane? Not with ten grand. He didn't know where he would go but it would not be back to a dosshouse bedsit. Anyway, two weeks was a long time. The game might only be starting.

Mrs Bradshaw had been housekeeper for the Rossettis for twenty years without ever forgetting her place. She was elderly and smiled a lot and was comfortable to have around. Monday to Friday, she cleaned, looked after the children when they were there, did the food shopping and cooked lunch.

She arrived, as always, at nine o'clock prompt, and would remain in the house until five. Maudie took the opportunity to take a nap upstairs.

He had acquired the habit of napping as he got older. As his life drifted away, his body had become less inclined to spend a large part of what was left sleeping.

It was not by choice that, back in the East End, he had sat awake in bed reading paperbacks and listening to the radio half the night. His mind refused to succumb to sleep. To compensate, he napped at odd times during the day, light snatches of slumber in the deckchair, from which he rose like a boxer at the ring of the shop bell.

He got up at ten thirty, teased the pain from his leg, showered and dressed with care. It was important to look the part. He wore the suit.

The old-fashioned cut-throat razor went into the inside pocket he had adjusted for the purpose. It was the only weapon he would carry. The shooter he had used the night before would stay at the house. If the Dysons retaliated, it would not be with violence in broad daylight. Only mugs carried shooters for show. If there was any trouble with the law, a razor could more easily be disposed of or explained .

The bouncer from the club had arrived at ten. He sat in the kitchen with the *Daily Mirror* crossword and a cup of coffee. He was a big lad in his late twenties, dressed in jeans and a sweatshirt that said Harvard.

"Good morning."

"Ah do, chief."

"You know what to do?"

"Aye. No one comes in unless t'old lady says so."

"You don't even open the door unless Mrs Bradshaw says so."

"Aye."

"Where's Miss Rossetti?"

"In t'study."

He knocked on the door, self-consciously, before entering. She was behind the desk. She had changed out of the shirt and jeans into more formal clothes, and looked a million dollars.

"Good rest?"

"Just the ticket. Where did you find the Harvard graduate?"

"Julian? He's from Barnsley. It's the third season he's been with us. He used to be a miner before they started closing the pits."

With a name like Julian it was no wonder he had left Barnsley, Maudie thought, then laughed at himself for his own name.

"Do you have somewhere I can put this?"

He held up a bundle wrapped in chamois leather that contained the gun and its accessories.

The far wall was half bookshelves and half cupboards. Toni opened one of the cupboards to reveal a safe. She opened its door and stepped aside to allow him to place the bundle on the middle shelf. She locked the safe, went back to the desk and wrote something on a slip of paper which she handed to him.

"The combination. In case I'm not around when you want it back."

It was another sign of trust, or there were two safes. Probably both. Toni wasn't daft. She wouldn't be so free with the combination of the one that really mattered.

"Are you ready?" he asked.

"Yes. I'll call a cab."

"No. We'll go in the Merc."

"Traffic's bad in the season. Nowhere to park."

"It doesn't matter. We'll park conspicuous and pay the tickets. Let them see us."

Chapter 14

TONI had dressed with care. Maudie had said the trip around town would be high profile so she made sure she looked the part.

A grey two-piece Chanel suit with Dior silk shirt in yellow. The high-heeled shoes and the tinted glasses were by Charles Jourdan.

She was worth looking at, if only for the labels. She knew plenty of women in town who would buy the labels from her – not the clothes, just the labels. The practice of stitching superior labels into inferior garments had, at one time, threatened to devalue exclusivity.

Toni drove. They went first to the hospital. She had told Mario only part of what she had planned. She was slightly worried about how he would take it when she told him everything. Well, almost everything.

The day was overcast and the the traffic heavy along North Park Drive, with cars queuing to turn into the zoo. The closer she got to the hospital, the faster the high dissipated.

Mario knew about Maudie. Or rather he knew that she had called in a favour and been loaned professional help. He didn't know the help was a volunteer who was past his best. It was time to introduce them.

Maudie waited in the corridor while she went in to Mario's room.

"You're looking better."

He did, too. He was still on his back but his shoulders

were raised on pillows and he held a copy of the *Daily Telegraph*. He lowered the paper.

"You look pleased with yourself," he said. "What've you been up to?"

She kissed him and sat in the chair by the bed. He folded the newspaper and pushed it away.

"Why are you reading that? You know you prefer the *Mirror*."

"Image. I'm in a private room." He said it without humour. "What've you been up to?"

She held up her hands.

"In good time. First, you. Have you seen Mr Simpson?"

"This morning. The left leg will mend but the right needs another operation."

"How bad?"

"Not bad. Three pins. I'll hardly notice them." He shrugged. "A slight limp. It'll make me look distinguished."

"When will they do it?"

"Next week. If it goes all right, I'll be home soon."

She was both pleased and anxious. Any operation worried her, even though Mario was making light of it. Three steel pins in his leg seemed a lot, to her.

"And now, sister, what have you been doing? It showed on your face when you came in. You've got a secret."

Toni grinned.

"I've got the share document back. Emilio's shares. And the books. Everything."

For a moment, expression left his face in surprise.

"Got them back? How? How much?"

"For exactly what the Dysons paid – nothing."

She explained. About Maudie and about what had happened the previous night, but without reference to the bedroom antics that had preceded the main event.

He remained silent throughout, too shocked at each dramatic disclosure to say anything. When she had finished, they stared at each other, she expectantly, he numb.

Retelling the events had rekindled the excitement and she took out a packet of St Moritz and the lighter. Bugger hospital regulations, she needed a cigarette.

By the time she had lit one, Mario's expression had changed to deep thought.

"Will it work?" he said.

"I don't know. But it's better than rolling over and playing dead."

"What about this bloke, Morgan? Is he good enough?"

"He's outside. I'll get him."

Maudie was leaning against the wall eating a packet of crisps. It was a stance that did not inspire confidence. He offered the packet when she got close.

"Curry flavour," he said.

"No thanks. Mario would like to meet you."

He put the crisps in his pocket and brushed his mouth for crumbs.

"Let's hope it doesn't cause a relapse," he said, and followed her into the room.

Toni introduced them and they shook hands and Mario looked past him at the door as if expecting, or hoping, for someone else as well.

He looked at Toni and she could see the cautious optimism seeping away fast. Perhaps the familiarity of the last few days had blinded her a little. From her brother's point of view, Maudie did not look a good bet.

"I do not mean this as a personal slight, Mr Morgan, but are you . . . it?"

Maudie stood, legs apart, hands held in front of him, and nodded.

"That is correct, Mr Rossetti."

"Toni. I think we had better talk some more . . ."

Maudie butted in.

"If you have reservations, I'd be obliged if you told me. It's my neck."

"Yes. Well. Look, Mr Morgan . . ."

"Maudie."

". . . Maudie. Aren't you getting on a bit for this sort of thing?"

"I've had a hard life, Mr Rossetti . . ."

"Mario."

". . . Mario. It's done two things. It's caused premature ageing and it's made me a right bastard."

"But on your own?"

"If you had wanted an army, you could have had an army. But armies tend to fight battles and this way is a subtler form of persuasion. Also, armies have a habit of occupying conquered territory after the war is over."

Toni's confidence began to regain ground. He was making a stronger case than she could have done.

"Listen. Don't worry," she said. "Maudie has things under control."

"Well . . ."

"There's no point in worrying," Maudie said. "It's too late to worry. It's started. I'm involved and you've made your stand. If I walk away now, you're finished. For better or worse, you're stuck with me."

It was a succinct summation of the situation. But Toni wished he had phrased it with a little more diplomacy.

Chapter 15

THEY headed back into town and the traffic got heavier. The clouds had thickened.

"Traffic is worse than normal because of the weather," she said. "If they can't sit on the beach, they take to their cars."

When they reached the Winter Gardens, hordes of aimless pedestrians added to the hazard.

At the club, Toni parked out front at his direction. They pushed open the door and disturbed a tousle-haired bouncer who looked like a retired prize fighter. He had the racing page of a tabloid open on the reception desk.

"Hello, Clancy."

"Morning, Miss Rossetti. The Doc's upstairs."

Jimmy Doc was pouring boiling water into a tea pot when they went into the office. He wore co-ordinated slacks, shirt and sweater in canary yellow and grey. Maudie thought he looked like he had escaped from an aviary.

"Clancy buzzed. Told me you'd arrived," he said.

He put the kettle down and Toni introduced them. Maudie liked his handshake and his eyes. The look wasn't devious. It was strong and enquiring.

"Do I pass?" Maudie said.

"I don't know. You're a wee bit old, maybe."

Maudie laughed.

"He's a professional, Jimmy," Toni said.

The Scot looked at her, nodded, and looked back at Maudie.

"Aye."

They drank tea and Toni and the Doc talked business and then the Doc told Maudie that his security suggestions had been implemented. Extra male staff, careful vetting at the door and all-night security after the club had closed.

"It's now up to the Dysons," Maudie said. "Of course, they may just leave us alone." He sipped the tea. "But if we want to stay healthy, we have to work on the assumption that they'll hit back. If they do, it won't be a punch-up in the club. It will be major.

"If they still hope to take over the business, they'll leave the property alone. That means main targets will be you two, top management. Mario's too public. But if all they want to do is make an example then anything could be hit, property as well as people. Just stay careful."

He looked at Jimmy Doc.

"I'll be staying close to Toni. You make sure you don't put yourself in a position where you could have an accident."

"That had occurred to me," Jimmy said. "My brother and cousin are coming down from Glasgow for a holiday. They arrive this afternoon." He smiled. "They're not professionals, but they are hardmen. And they're young."

Maudie allowed him his smile.

Fat Gerard sweated a lot. He was overweight and the office was stuffy, but Maudie recognised that a percentage of the sweat was fear.

He was the third and last of the bingo hall managers they had seen and Maudie did not think it would be politic to stress the dangers in the same terms as he had with the Doc.

"Nothing might happen," he told him. "If it does, it's more likely to be at the club than here or one of the other halls. Just be careful. First sign of trouble get on the blower to the old bill."

"Don't worry. I will."

"Have you arranged night security?"

"Yes. There'll be someone in the hall every night."

"Good. Tell them no heroics. If anyone tries to get in, they get on the phone." Gerard nodded and licked his lips. "And watch out yourself. Have a few early nights. Go straight home by taxi."

"What about Toni?"

"Toni will be all right. I'll be with Toni."

He nodded again as if reassured but he still looked nervous.

Toni exhaled tobacco smoke into the pause.

"Will you be all right, Gerard?" she asked.

"Don't be daft, you silly bitch. Course I will. I'll be careful. You look after yourself." He cast a glance at Maudie. "Make sure grandad takes his Phyllosan. You don't want him falling asleep when the trouble starts."

Maudie laughed. The remark reminded him that he still hadn't had the opportunity to visit a chemist.

Toni said, "Just take care, Gerard."

"Don't sodding worry. Any bother and I'll be legging it up to Montague Street nick. Olympic time, no starting blocks. It'll be a red-hot poker up the arse job."

The sun was breaking through when they left the bingo hall.

"The weather's the wrong way round," Toni said as they got in the car.

"What do you mean? The sun's out. That has to be good news."

"Not for traders. They want the sun early in the

morning to get the trippers here and on the beach, then a good cloudburst about eleven o'clock to drive them into the cafes and arcades."

"The sort of summers we have, it's no wonder there are still fortunes to be made."

"Blackpool is the only resort geared to the Great British Summer. It can rain every day of your holiday and there's always something to do."

"At a price."

"Of course at a price. Everything has a price."

She took him to a pub called The Union for lunch. It was far enough from the Promenade to escape the crowds.

Ten minutes after they had arrived, Ruth walked in, exchanged a joke with the landlord, and noticed them as if by chance.

"Have you been sending invitations?" Maudie asked Toni.

"She called this morning when you were asleep and wouldn't be put off. I thought this would be the safest way to see her."

"Keep it light and distant," he said, standing as Ruth arrived.

"Oh, a perfect gentleman," she said.

"I'm going to the chemist."

"Really?"

She raised her eyebrows suggestively and he felt foolish.

"For shampoo. And you need your backside smacking."

"Promises, promises."

He left them and went outside. Toni would be okay for five minutes. He had noticed a chemist's shop a few doors away when they arrived.

He bought two different products that professed to do

the same job, one a spray, the other a cream. He also bought shampoo.

They returned to the house before two o'clock. Julian let them in without comment.

"What now?" Toni asked.

"I'm going to have a nap. You freshen up. Later you can go shopping."

"I don't need anything."

"It doesn't matter. We are going to be seen around town. I'll carry the parcels and look like George Raft."

"Who?"

"Clint Eastwood."

His leg tightened up again during the nap and he used the cream before they left for a high-profile afternoon. It seemed to help. The penetrating heat had a definite beneficial effect.

Toni entered into the spirit of the shopping trip when she realised she could have fun. It consisted of making him uncomfortable by leaving him standing outside ladies' changing rooms, or asking his opinion about intimate garments in lingerie shops.

The sun had decided to stay out and once again he regretted the solid craftsmanship of the woollen suit. She noticed his discomfort and insisted that if he was going to wear a suit, he should have one of lightweight material.

Despite his opposition, she took him to the men's department of C&A's and chose a two piece, single breasted, light grey summerweight suit.

The way she fussed, he began to think the impression she was creating was that he was her father rather than her minder. He knew she was doing it on purpose and he agreed to try it on, and to let her buy it, to humour her and escape the attention.

When they were outside, she laughed.

"Come on. You've suffered enough," she said.

She took him through a restaurant busy with holidaymakers, upstairs to a coffee lounge with views of the sea through floor-to-ceiling double glazing.

Conversations were conducted in a murmur, tea, coffee and cakes were served by waitresses in black dresses and white aprons that he remembered from Joe Lyons days, and the customers appeared to be mainly local and well off.

It was a pleasant interlude, despite the weight of the suit. Down below, the beach was full of small family camps, colourful deckchairs and windbreakers marking perimeter lines. Escapers splashed in the sea.

"Can you smell something?" Toni asked.

"What?"

"A funny smell. Sort of antiseptic."

He could smell something. The deep-heat cream. He crossed his legs away from her.

"Cleaning fluid," he said. "Somebody's spilled something and they've cleaned it up."

When they returned to the house, Maudie took a shower and washed off the liniment. He would suffer the pain rather than the embarrassment.

That night they dined out in a seafood restaurant in South Shore. Later, they made an appearance at Dolly's. It was brief and almost formal. Like a royal visit.

Finally they went back to the house for the last time and relieved Julian, who took a taxi home.

Maudie checked the interior of the house and then outside, with the floodlights on and Toni keeping brick-chewing Paolo under control.

Back inside, they switched on the burglar alarm.

"End of a perfect day," he said.

"Perfect?"

"No one got hurt."

"And so to bed?"

Maudie nodded.

"And the world service."

Chapter 16

NOTHING happened for three days. They kept up appearances around town, and Toni and Jimmy Doc and his relatives relaxed visibly as time progressed. But Maudie became more uncomfortable, despite the lightweight suit. So far it had been a phony war. A lot of bluster and one victim. Now it felt like a phony peace.

The weather remained hot and oppressive and his leg continued to ache. Not all the time, but first thing after a nap or after he had been walking for a while without a rest. He used the deep-heat potions at night and washed them off in the morning.

Jimmy Doc phoned on Sunday lunchtime. Maudie took the call.

"There was trouble at Riley's last night," Jimmy said. "A crowd of Scots, down from Stirling for the weekend. The bouncers over-reacted a wee bit."

"Will the Dysons have trouble with the police?"

"It's possible. It depends. The lads were kicked out of Riley's. Then Dysons' heavy mob followed them and badly damaged them well away from the club. The lads themselves might not tell the police. The code of the hardmen."

"Perhaps someone can drop a hint in the right ear."

That night, the phony peace ended.

They had watched a late-night film together on television. When Toni went to bed, Maudie settled into an armchair with a paperback and world service radio.

The telephone rang at ten past one and Maudie answered it. The voice at the other end was without expression.

"There's a present on the back lawn."

The line went dead.

The .38 Smith and Wesson, with the silencer already fitted, lay on the table alongside a pair of surgical gloves in a cellophane packet. Maudie put on the gloves, picked up the gun and went to the kitchen where he switched on the lights to illuminate the back garden.

He retraced his steps into the hall and went upstairs. Toni was standing in the doorway of her room, wearing jeans and a sweater. She had taken to going to bed prepared for sudden eventualities.

"I heard the phone."

He nodded and led the way into the bedroom he had been using. It overlooked the back garden.

"Close the door," he said, when she followed him in. "Don't switch on the light. They said there's something on the lawn."

The curtains were open and they stood side by side in the darkness and looked out. At the far end of the lawn was a large bundle of what appeared to be old clothes. It rolled over and they saw it was a man.

"Oh, my God." Toni moved closer to the window. "It's Gerard."

Maudie's mouth went dry and butterflies began to mate in his stomach. His leg began to throb. Had it just started or had he only noticed it now he knew he was required to take action?

Gerard was lying on his side. His hands were tied behind his back and, from the way his legs were bent, they were also tied to his ankles. He lay in a shapeless lump. His stomach stretched his shirt like an overstuffed sandbag. He was totally motionless.

There was no movement from anywhere in the garden.

Where was Paolo? Why hadn't the dog raised the alarm when the intruders had brought Gerard over the wall?

He scanned the two greenhouses at the side of the long lawn, and the garden shed at the far end. No shadows moved. The shrubbery was still. But where was Paolo? Poisoned meat?

"Where's your shooter?" he asked.

"In the bedroom."

"Get it."

When she returned carrying it, he noticed she was wearing tan leather gloves. She had remembered his advice. They went downstairs.

Toni switched off the burglar alarm and Maudie put on his jacket. He would need the razor in its inside pocket to cut Gerard free. He led the way to the side door that led into the garage. Jane trotted at their heels.

"Stay back," he said to Toni.

He opened the door and let the kitchen light spill into the garage.

"Go, Jane!" he said.

The white bull terrier went into the garage on a hunt and they listened to her sniffing around.

When he was satisfied, he reached around the jamb and switched on the internal garage lights. He was reassured when they came on. It indicated that no one was inside.

None the less, he took his time making sure that the garage and the two cars, Mario's Merc and Angie's Honda, held no uninvited visitors.

"It's okay," he told Toni.

She stepped into the kitchen doorway, the Mauser automatic in her right hand. He went to the door that led from the garage into the back garden.

"Turn the lights off and come here." She did so and by the time she had joined him, he had unbolted and unlocked the outer door. "Lock it behind me. Then go into the house and lock the kitchen door, too. Take Jane with you. Switch the alarm back on. I'll bring Gerard to the french windows. Don't switch the alarm off until I get there. Okay?"

Her face was tense but determined.

"Okay."

He smiled.

"It'll be all right, gel. I won't be long."

She smiled back and some of the tension went.

Maudie opened the door and stepped outside, the gun held at his side. The key turned in the lock behind him and the two bolts snapped home.

He remained standing against the wall and stared into the darkness of the shrubbery and the greenhouse rather than at the illuminated lawn.

Nothing moved.

He shivered. Standing around like this made him feel the cold. He went along the path that went through trellised arches covered in climbing roses. There were three arches and at each one he paused to look and listen.

Still nothing but normal night sounds and the rustle of a breeze in the trees.

Where was Paolo?

He reached the first greenhouse and tried the door. It was locked, the key on the outside. The second greenhouse was the same. He waited with his back against it and, for the first time, gave his attention to Gerard.

The obese bingo manager was unconscious. The ropes that bound him did not look tight but they were incapacitating. It was doubtful, because of his size, that Gerard's hands could be made to meet each other behind his back. His captors had settled for a four- or five-inch linking rope that was also attached to his ankles. He would be unable to straighten his legs and, with his cumbersome shape, he would be unable to move very much, if at all.

The garden remained peaceful. The tied body was a contradiction.

Gerard lay like a prize exhibit under the garden

spotlights. He was the Dysons' reply that the challenge had been accepted. It had been inevitable. He had only been fooling himself with the hope that they would lose bottle and back off. There was no way they could afford to.

At this distance, Gerard did not look badly hurt. But Maudie knew from experience that his trousers could contain all manner of mischief.

He took the razor from its inside pocket and stepped on to the lawn.

Still quiet.

Where was the bloody dog?

Maudie knelt on his right knee, his left leg complaining despite the care with which he made the manoeuvre, and he sensed the danger a second before it arrived.

He tried to push himself sideways so he could roll to safety and cover himself with the gun, but the damned leg let him down.

It gave way, and tilted his body obligingly towards the danger instead of away from it.

He felt the blow and the inside of his head momentarily exploded. The illuminations had come early, but they didn't last long. They were engulfed in blackness.

Chapter 17

TONI watched it happen from the bedroom. It gave her a grandstand view until it was time to open the french window.

Maudie's progress had been so slow she had wanted to shout at him to get a move on, to go directly to Gerard and bring him into the safety of the house.

She concentrated on staying calm, but found it difficult.

He knows what he's doing. There's a reason for being so cautious, she told herself. Someone might still be out there.

She knew all the reasons but they didn't help. She was racked by guilt at Gerard being hurt and trussed like a turkey. She wanted him inside the house, untied and with a whisky in his hand. She wanted him to reassure her he was fine and that she was not to blame.

And where was Paolo?

Another pang of guilt.

They had probably drugged the dog with a piece of meat. She had seen it all on television. The animal would wake up with a sore head in the morning.

Then Maudie walked across the lawn and knelt stiffly by Gerard's side. He paused for a moment and she saw the two shadows run silently from the far side of the garden shed.

Her mouth opened in horror but no sound came out. It was too late.

One swing of a cosh and Maudie slumped across the body of Gerard. They didn't waste time. They picked him up between them and carried him back the way they had come. It took only seconds.

The garden was empty again, except for Gerard, who was still tied and motionless in the middle of the well-lit lawn.

She was numb. The whole scenario was as unreal as that same television thriller where the dog was drugged. She looked around for reassurance but found none.

This had once been Mario's room, before he married. The room was real. The furniture was where it had always been and even the smells were the same. An old dampness combined with Mrs Bradshaw's particular brand of polish. The garden was real, too. So was Gerard.

God. What had they done to Gerard? What would they do to Maudie?

The guilt was overwhelming until she realised her own vulnerability.

She was alone in the house. Her fingers curled possessively around the butt of the gun and she lifted it closer to her face to inspect it in the half light. It was on safety. She pushed the catch off and on again, to reassure herself how easy it was to arm the weapon.

Be rational, she told herself.

The house is securely locked and the alarm system is switched on. I have a gun and a dog. I am not helpless and I am not at risk.

She looked out of the window again, at Gerard.

Nowhere near as at risk as her unconscious fat friend or her old-age professional.

What should she do? The garden was full of shadows that had already dealt with a guard dog and Maudie. Should she call the police? Jimmy Doc?

Jimmy Doc. She would get him round here with his relatives and any other muscle he could muster.

By the time she got to the top of the stairs, the hall telephone was ringing.

"Hello?"

She recognised the voice that laughed slowly at the other end of the line. It belonged to the thug who had threatened her outside the casino with a Stanley knife.

"What do you want?"

"Now there's a leading question."

"Get to the point."

"The point is, you are all alone now that grandad's out of the way."

"Don't hurt him."

"Hurt grandad? Course not. He's just having a little trip. Be away a couple of days. You won't recognise him when you get him back." He laughed and his voice became suddenly menacing. "Unless you start behaving like a lady."

"What does that mean?"

"Oh, I'm not trusted with business. Someone else will talk to you tomorrow about that. I'm just involved in security. Your security."

"Make sure he's safe or there'll be no point talking tomorrow."

"He'll be safe." The voice became a leer. "You should worry about yourself."

Her skin crawled. Even the anger didn't help. It was a blatant sexual threat.

"I'll be fine."

"I hope so, but . . ."

She hated herself but she had to ask.

"But what?"

"Well. We're supposed to make sure no one bothers you. A good-looking woman, all alone in a big house."

"I have a gun."

"Oh dear. I'm terrified. The thing is, the help you get these days is so unreliable. Take Melvyn. You know Melvyn. You met him at the casino. Not face to face, but I'm sure he made an impression. He certainly remembers you. He's told us all about you. How you felt under your skirt. How soft you were. How wet you were . . ."

"You bastard. You juvenile pervert. Are you getting off on this? Got your willie in your hand? You're pathetic. If I see you again I'll give you a memory. A bullet in the balls. Tell Melvyn that goes for him, too."

She slammed down the receiver, tears damping her eyes. It couldn't even be straight violence with them. It had to be sexual violence. Dominance of the species. Did they think she would faint away at the thought of rape? Poor little frightened woman?

The phone rang again and made her jump. She counted the rings to calm herself. On ten, she picked it up.

"My, my. What a temper."

"This has gone far enough. I think it's time I called the police."

"I don't think that's a good idea. If you did, grandad might not survive his trip. And anyway, you won't be able to. Your telephone line will be cut as soon as we finish talking."

She had lived with the threat of extreme violence for the last two weeks. The possibility of someone being killed in the crossfire had been a consideration she had put firmly out of her mind before it could settle. But now it had been said. Maudie could be the one to die. It stunned her.

"I've told you. He must not be hurt."

"And I've told you. That will depend."

She listened to his breathing, unable to think of anything worthwhile to say. There was nothing to say that would make any difference now. She would have to wait until daylight and the inevitable approach from the Dysons to sell out.

"Are you still there?" The leer had returned. "Melvyn wanted to send his regards. He'd very much like to see you again, face to face." He laughed. "Or not necessarily face to face. He quite liked the last time. And he's got some of the other lads worked up. So I hope the doors . . ."

She broke the connection. This time she couldn't stop the tears. They were tears of anger, she told herself, and tried to make the anger dominant. But they were also caused by frustration, guilt, failure and fear. A large part fear.

Her helplessness outside the casino had been total. She had been unable to move because of the knife at her face while the hands moved nauseatingly beneath her skirt. It would not happen again.

The telephone. Had they carried out their threat to cut it? Did she have time to call Jimmy Doc?

It was dead. She was isolated.

"Come on, Jane."

The dog trotted by her side into the study and sat and waited while she peeled off her gloves and poured herself a large vodka and tonic.

"Cheers."

Toni toasted her and gulped down half the drink.

How predictable. Run to the bottle at times of stress. She taunted herself, finished the drink and poured another. All the best heroes drank. But they were heroes. In a woman, it was judged to be a weakness.

The vodka either steadied her nerves or numbed them. She didn't know or care which. It also fuelled her anger and built her confidence. She went from room to room on the ground floor, and switched on every light.

The gun remained in her ungloved right hand. If she shot one of these bastards she now wanted the credit, not anonymity.

Jane stayed by her side when she went back upstairs to Maudie's darkened bedroom to stand in the shadows by the window and look into the garden.

Gerard hadn't moved. He lay as if in a deep sleep. She hoped it would last until morning. Leaving the house to attempt to free him would be madness. He would remain tied and she would be raped.

He could not be badly hurt, she told herself. She so much wanted to believe it that she did.

They had threatened Maudie. That implied no one had yet been seriously hurt. Gerard would be stiff and sore in the morning, nothing worse. But staring at him would not help. It would just cloud her judgment and she needed objectivity for survival.

She could not go out until the morning. If she valued Maudie's life she could not attract the police by firing the gun out of the window or by setting off the alarm. Because the telephone was cut she could summon no other help. She had to remain alert and she had to keep the house secure.

One advantage she had was that they, too, would not wish to set off the burglar alarm and attract the police. But they were criminals. Perhaps they could beat the system? Cut out the alarm?

"Come on, Jane."

The silence appeared to be holding its breath as she walked back to the study and poured another vodka. She had to be careful to keep the intake under control. Enough to maintain courage, not enough to become drunk.

The bastards would not make her crack tonight. They would not beat her because of the darkness and loneliness and because she was a woman.

She pushed the safety catch of the Mauser to off.

Chapter 18

THE house creaked. In other circumstances they would have been friendly sounds of age and familiarity. Now they fuelled fear.

Toni moved from room to room downstairs, unable to settle. The silence was oppressive, the creaks harbingers of terror.

She turned on the radio and immediately switched it off again. The imperfect silence was preferable to distraction. She had to be able to hear any attempts at breaking in.

Instead, she turned on the television in the living room and inserted a video. Mario Lanza without the sound. The colour and people were company. She sat on the sofa and invited Jane to jump up and join her. The white bull terrier was comforting and she stroked its powerful neck and chest.

Had she been totally wrong to attempt what she had? Had she had the right to put other people at risk? It would have been inconceivable to have buckled under immediately and sold out. So was it simply pride that had made her think she could fight back and win? A gesture of defiance that had now put Maudie's life on the line? A gesture rather than real defiance?

Mario had felt the argument of violence first and was still on his back. His lesson had cost him pain and a limp for life. He had been ready to be persuaded to sell, not to save himself more pain but to save others from being hurt.

The responsibility for Gerard and Maudie was hers. So where did she go now? Sell out to save Maudie? To save anyone else getting hurt?

Why should she worry? There were daily flights to America.

The tapping at the window made her start. The bull terrier's head snapped up, its ears pricked for action. The tapping continued and the dog jumped to the floor, ran to the curtain and stood growling, the hair bristling on its neck.

Toni picked up the gun and took a hestitant step towards the window. The voice stopped her. It was a whisper of menace, yet she strained to hear what it said.

"Toni. Toni Rossetti. We're waiting. Unlock the door and get it over with. There are only four of us. You can manage four of us, can't you? Two at a time. Maybe three. Shall I tell you what we're going to do . . ."

She pointed the gun, her arm trembling. The voice droned on in obscenities but she was no longer listening. The tremble in her arm had spread to her whole body. It was just talk, they hadn't attempted to get in. Just talk. The time to shoot was when, if, they tried to get in.

Toni backed to the door into the corridor, feeling her way past the furniture, the gun still pointing at the unseen speaker. The dog remained, puzzled but on guard, sitting down to watch the curtain. Toni went back to the study, back to the vodka.

This time she sipped the drink instead of gulping. It was important not to go to pieces, to stay in control. She remained in the study doorway, looking along the corridor to the open door of the living room. The gun in one hand, the drink in the other. If anything happened, she would know and she would be ready.

After an eternity, Jane came trotting out of the room,

looking for her. The dog had calmed down. The danger was past.

Toni had crouched to fuss the animal when the tapping started again. They both looked up, the dog expectantly and Toni with a feeling of horror.

They went into the large circular reception hall. There were two sets of double glass doors opposite each other. The doors to the left led into the stone-flagged entrance porch and to the front door. The doors to the right led into a small unused conservatory and the french windows into the garden. Both sets of doors were curtained. The sound was coming from the french windows and, although muffled by the intervening conservatory, was still audible. The message was the same.

She retreated once more to the study to retrieve her drink but restrained herself from even sipping it. It was there if she needed it. At the moment she did not need it. She carried it into the living room and watched the silent tenor with determination.

The drink lasted half an hour and she was contemplating getting another when she heard muffled footsteps outside. Both she and the dog stiffened.

Two men were whispering at the back of the house. Two? Perhaps it was four. The voice had said four. More footsteps, soft but distinct, and a repressed laugh. Lascivious? In anticipation?

Toni controlled her trembling and tried to avoid thoughts of gang rape, of brutal men imposing themselves upon her. It was kidology. A male fantasy with which to frighten her. Sex for men was always domination. Well, this time the domination would not come cheap.

"Two girls together, Jane." She stroked the dog. "Go for their balls, girl."

Jane grunted in her throat and licked Toni's hand.

They sat on the sofa, sharing the tension, listening to the movement and indistinct voices outside for more than ten minutes. Then the sounds stopped as abruptly as they had begun and the silence returned.

She felt drained and incapable of movement. She remained sitting, one arm round the dog, the gun held limply in her other hand. The video finished and the screen filled with static. When the cassette reached the end, the machine clicked into reverse to rewind the tape.

The noise attracted her attention. The digital clock said it was twelve minutes past three. When the tape had fully rewound, she got up and pressed the play button again.

It was silly but she wanted to go to bed. She was tired. Jane had already gone to sleep and she had had enough. The bastards out there could continue to play out their wet dreams but she wanted to go to bed.

The front doorbell's ring was totally unexpected.

She dropped the empty glass and it fell unbroken on to the carpet. The ring was loud and long. A pause and it rang again. And again. Insistent. Anxious for a reply.

It could be Jimmy Doc. Or Ruth? If they had tried to telephone they could have become worried at being unable to get through.

She ran down the corridor into the hall, her sudden movement energising the dog into following her. At the curtains she hesitated. What if it wasn't Jimmy Doc? What if it was them?

They could already be waiting in the entrance hall beyond the curtains. Would the glass doors be protection enough?

There was nothing to be gained in delay. She checked that the entrance porch light was switched on, and swept back the curtains.

The ringing stopped.

The porch was empty apart from the wooden bench and the two giant vases. The light was harsh and she screwed her eyes to see if she could recognise the figure beyond the glass and wrought-iron outer door. All she could tell was that it was male.

The figure stooped, pushed a small package through the letter box, and walked off out of sight.

Toni tried to gather thoughts that had been slugged with disappointment. It was not Jimmy Doc. It was them. Her gaze fixed upon the package.

Was this the offer from the Dysons? Their ultimatum. It could be one of Maudie's fingers. God, she was falling apart, back with the television plot.

It wouldn't be long to dawn and nothing had happened. Nothing would happen. It was all calculated pressure.

She unlocked the double doors and levelled the gun. A deep breath and she went into the entrance hall. Two, three paces. She bent close to the front door to pick up the package, half expecting a face to appear or an axe to come crashing through a glass panel.

Nothing happened. The outside darkness remained undisturbed and she returned swiftly through the double doors, locked them and pulled the curtains closed.

Her breathing was ragged and she felt it was time for another vodka. The dog followed her into the study where she wondered what had happened to her glass. She used a clean one and sat at the desk. The gun, the glass and the package were laid out before her.

It was a white envelope, the size of a cigarette case. She took a drink and then tore off the end of the envelope and slid out a thin cardboard box of the sort used by cheap jewellery shops. She placed the box carefully in front of her and removed the lid.

They lay side by side. Four of them. Pink and limp and used. Four skin-like sheaths, sheened with slime. It took a long second for realisation to penetrate. When it did she felt sick.

She picked up the gun and ran upstairs, into her

bedroom, and threw herself on to the bed. This time she didn't try to stop the tears because she couldn't stop her imagination.

Men, faces heavy with lust, saliva glinting in open mouths, hiding in the darkness outside. Trousers open, hands busy, preparing the message.

Men, prying open windows, picking locks, silently entering the house. Silent but for their breathing. Panting like animals. Fingers crooked to rip off her clothes, to pull at her body. Climbing the stairs to find her.

"God!"

She pummelled the pillow and buried her sobs in its softness. She was tired. They had pushed her into their fantasy and she was almost lost. They had turned her into a wreck. But she had to fight it. Despite the tiredness. Wouldn't they laugh if they could see the state she was in? She sniffled to stop the tears and lay still in exhaustion.

And heard the panting.

Her body froze and the only sensation she felt was fear causing turmoil in her stomach and then spreading throughout her body.

Someone was by the door behind her. The shallow panting was the focus of her terror. He wasn't moving. He was standing watching her.

Where was the gun? Why had she let go of the gun?

She opened her right eye and looked along the pillow. The gun was beside her hand. Close enough to reach. Was that why he hesitated in the doorway?

She grabbed hold of it and rolled on to her back, pointing the weapon and screaming.

Jane barked and jumped on the bed and she almost shot her.

There was no man. There was nobody.

The dog stood over her, stiff legged with eagerness.

Tail wagging, tongue lolling. Breath panting. It licked her face.

She dropped the gun and embraced the dog, crying and laughing at the same time. It was insane. They had pushed her far enough. If they wanted to break in, they could. She would give them a welcome they would not forget.

The panic had gone and she felt calm and in control again. Her mind was once more working logically. She went into Maudie's room and looked into the garden. Gerard lay still on the lawn, his head now tilted to one side, still peaceful.

The false dawn of early summer would soon be here and it would be light enough to make them retreat and leave her alone. She would fix her face. If anyone did see her, she didn't want them to know she had been crying.

She washed her face and brushed her teeth and sat at the dressing table to apply fresh make-up, taking her time, making a good job of it. If she had to shoot someone, she wanted to look good when she did it.

There were no doubts now that she would use the gun. When Maudie had first handed it to her, she had wondered whether she would ever have the nerve to pull the trigger in anger. Now she knew there would be no hesitation, no compunction. Her tormentors were animals.

The make-up job was complete. She looked in the mirror and admired her skill rather than her looks. She blew herself a kiss. She had survived the night.

The banging started when she was halfway down the stairs. Loud banging from the rear of the house, as if someone was using a hammer against a door.

Her anger blazed and she went quickly through the house to the kitchen. The noise was coming from the rear door of the garage that led into the garden.

"Ready, Jane!"

The urgency in her voice communicated to the dog. It barked and bristled.

Toni followed Maudie's procedure and unlocked the door from the kitchen into the garage. She pushed it open and stepped back to cover it with the gun.

"Go, Jane!"

The dog went in and ran straight to the outer door. The bangs were louder now and the bull terrier bounced and barked.

Toni looked into the garage and switched the light on. It seemed as empty as before. She pointed the gun at the back door and fired. The sound was magnified in the echo chamber of brick and concrete. The single shot splintered the wood and the banging stopped. Jane looked round in surprise.

"Come on, you bastards. Come and get it."

Silence, then footsteps running.

"Jane. Come here, girl."

The dog came back into the kitchen and Toni relocked the door. For the first time since the siege had begun, she felt good. She had taken positive action and got a positive result. Soon she would be able to go into the garden and cut Gerard free. She put the kettle on and, while she waited for it to boil, she tidied up.

The used contraceptives were tipped into the lavatory and flushed away, the box and its envelope put into the wastebin. The glasses were washed and the vodka bottle replaced. She switched off the static-screened television.

The tea was refreshing and she refilled her cup and took it upstairs to the bedroom. Outside it was now fully light, although still too early for people to be up and about. But there were no longer any shadows and the hazy brightness of the sun lifted her spirits. It was time to go for Gerard.

Downstairs she went from room to room, turning out the lights and opening curtains. There were no signs of the faceless men who had prowled the grounds during the night.

Everything looked so normal that the horrors she had so recently experienced were already taking on the aspects of a bad dream rather than reality.

"Come on, Jane. Let's go see Gerard."

She unlocked the door into the garage, following the now set precautions. Jane wagged her tail. She sensed no danger and ran to the outer door eagerly and began to sniff and scratch at its base, eager for a run.

Toni unbolted the door and mentally prepared herself. She half hoped they were still out there. In the daylight she would have a clear shot. It would be good to pay them back. She pulled the door open . . . and screamed.

The thing was coming at her at head height and she stepped back, raised the gun and fired and fired and fired. Only one of the bullets hit but it didn't matter. Paolo, the second bull terrier, was already very dead.

"Oh no."

The dog had been nailed to the frame above the door. Its head, chest and forelegs hung in the open space. Its head was at a strange angle because its throat had been cut. Blood had dripped on to the path below. Jane was curiously sniffing and licking at the partially congealed pool.

Toni slumped back against the side of the Mercedes. She didn't have the motivation to shout at Jane to stop. She was totally filled with a dull anger that would only be assuaged by revenge. She wanted to hurt them back, to physically inflict pain, to make them scream.

There was a box of cloths and dusters at the back of the garage and she pushed Jane away and used them to cover the pool of blood. Then she walked without hesitation into the garden and on to the lawn.

As she approached Gerard she could hear him snoring. There couldn't be much wrong with a man who snored.

She bent over him and shook him but he remained unconscious. A handful of downers and a half bottle of whisky and he would have been no trouble to anybody. He smelled. He had peed his trousers during the night.

The thick cord held him loosely but securely. She used the kitchen scissors to cut and unravel it. Even then he didn't wake up. She began to straighten his legs and arms and he rolled over into a more comfortable position of his own accord, and continued sleeping.

Toni stood up, looked around the garden and back to the house. She still had Paolo to deal with. She would bury him down here, at the edge of the lawn.

There was plenty of time. They had gone. It was over. For now.

Chapter 19

MAUDIE'S hangover was king sized. And then he remembered it wasn't a hangover.

He hurt all over. His head from the blow and his limbs from being held in unnatural positions by rope. Like Gerard's, his arms were tied behind his back and attached to his ankles, which were hobbled. They had not been as kind with him as they had with the bingo manager. His ropes were tight.

He was lying on a concrete floor. The place was dark and cool. It could have been a garage or a cellar. The ropes allowed no possibility of escape. He should save his energy and try to avoid thinking of the growing pain in his arms and legs, particularly his legs. He shifted position slightly for comfort but didn't find any. Shit. He should think of better times. Like being in prison.

His reactions had been slow, not to mention his brain. He shouldn't have gone into the garden alone and at night. He should have telephoned for reinforcements or waited until morning. But being around Toni had made him soft. He had gone out on a solo rescue mission for her benefit. Or was it to prove how tough he was after so many days of inactivity? Change that. Make it years of inactivity.

But self-recrimination was self-defeating. He was here, now, and in a mess with all the signs indicating that it could develop into a bigger mess.

The Dysons had several options, all of them unpleasant, as far as he was concerned. They could warn him off, hold him until they had forced a deal, or severely damage him. He realised that 'severely' could be open to wide interpretation.

There was no point dwelling upon it. Whichever they picked would be painful to some degree. He tried to relax as much as possible, tried to persuade his limbs that the ropes were extra tendons and natural confinements. He relaxed into his bonds instead of tensing his muscles against them. After a while, he even dozed.

The light awakened him. He opened his eyes and saw that the building was a warehouse. Footsteps approached.

"Morning, grandad. Hope you slept well."

The voice was nondescript and conversational, the accent north of Spaghetti Junction but no more definite than that.

The man stopped in front of him and crouched on his haunches to look into his face. He had fair hair, cut short, even features that hadn't been marked, and he smiled to show his teeth. White and even. The lad was either good to carry no scars and retain his teeth or he was new to the game.

"Are you the best she could get?" He shook his head. "It's no contest. You should have been content with your pension."

A door banged and the man looked over his shoulder.

"Is he conscious?"

"Yes."

More footsteps, brisk and healthy, echoing towards them. Maudie, his face against the concrete, could feel them reverberating in his head.

A pair of black lace-up shoes and neatly pressed black trousers stopped alongside the first man. Maudie refused to give them the satisfaction of looking up to see who it was.

"Untie his legs and prop him up."

Maudie gasped as his legs were straightened and

circulation was restored. The pain was intense but he tried not to let it show. The blond-haired man sat him against the wall, his hands still tied behind him.

The one who had given the order looked at him with frank curiosity. He was tall and lean, early forties. He wore a white shirt and a grey cashmere sweater with the black trousers. Sort of formal leisurewear.

"I'm Paul Unsworth. We made enquiries about you. You used to be good."

It was meant as a compliment with no edge and no sarcasm. They exchanged looks. He was a pro. Cold eyes but no malice. He could as easily break the legs of a close friend as those of a total stranger. Unsworth. Head of security, according to Toni. He looked extremely capable.

"You shouldn't have come," Unsworth said. "The odds were wrong."

He took out a packet of Rothmans, put a cigarette in his mouth and lit it. He offered the pack.

Maudie shook his head.

"I gave up."

Unsworth nodded.

"Very wise." He took a drag of the cigarette. "Did you miss the action?"

"Something like that."

He nodded again.

"Graham. Get Mr Morgan some tea and toast. And when you bring it, be careful. Tie his feet before you untie his hands, and stay out of reach." He smiled at Maudie. "Don't do anything silly. The odds are still wrong."

Unsworth left through a side door into another room. The warehouse had windows and was lit by fluorescent lights.

"As the man said, don't try anything silly," Graham said, and produced a Stanley knife. He held it in front of Maudie's face. "Stanley wouldn't like it."

Maudie gave him a tired smile.

"As the man said, go and get the tea and toast. There's a good lad."

Graham's grin faltered and Maudie knew he would have loved to have cut him. But that was outside his range of orders and this was a lad who looked as if he was good at obeying orders.

"Later." He sniggered while still showing his teeth. Maudie thought he must be really proud of them. "I'll have you later."

He got up and walked towards the side door.

"Melvyn!"

The door opened and a squat, heavy youth with lank dark hair came in. He carried a baseball bat. Maudie wondered where he had got it. It was not an everyday piece of equipment and showed a touch of flamboyant amateurism.

Graham said, "Watch grandad. Any problem, rupture a kidney."

Over breakfast they made fun of the rubber gloves he wore, suggesting he did so because of a fetish rather than professionalism.

When he had finished, they tied him again but thankfully didn't return him to the oven-ready position. He was left to sit against the wall with his hands in front of him. At least he could see his watch. Melvyn or Graham remained with him in turn, sitting in a canvas garden chair. No chance presented itself.

"I want to pee," he said to Melvyn, when the two of them were alone.

"So pee."

The Dyson brothers came at eleven thirty. There was no mistaking Eric. He was plump and exuded all the charm of a bent accountant. Paul Unsworth and another man were with them.

The new man was stacked with muscles that his suit struggled to contain. His hair was shaved to a close crop, his nose broken, and Maudie bet he had hate and love tattooed on his knuckles. He had the glare of a psychopath and Maudie speculated that this was Carl Curtis, the other security import from Manchester, who had served a five for manslaughter.

What was wrong with today's parole boards? One look should have been enough for them to have thrown away the key. Graham and Melvyn looked definitely third division in this company.

The group of four walked over to inspect him silently. Eric pursed his lips and Maudie wondered whether he might be bent the other way, too. Curtis simply glared, impersonal and deadly. Maudie had seen his kind before. They were a liability in the long run, just like Ronnie Kray had been. There was only one way to deal with them. Take them off at the knees. Then at the neck.

Steven Dyson smiled maliciously.

"We meet again."

Maudie said nothing. Verbal heroics were for mugs and amateurs. He kept his eyes lowered.

Steven went on. "Tell me. I'm curious. Why did you come? You're too old. What made you try? It couldn't have been the money. Perhaps you were getting fringe benefits. Were you? Was Toni Rossetti letting you fuck her?"

He kept looking at his feet. There was no point getting angry. They were only words.

Steven laughed.

"I must admit, she is good. She's so good, I've decided to share her with Melvyn and Graham here. And Carl. I think Carl will like her. After being inside he has peculiar habits. I'm sure she'll appreciate them."

Maudie slowly looked up and locked his eyes on those of Steven Dyson. Looks can't kill and he kept his face neutral. But it was a diversion that made Dyson change tack.

"God knows what she sees in you. She's so eager to get

you back she's ready to sell. But do you know something? That's not enough. I want more. We want more." He smiled. "You're going to hurt. You're going to hurt a lot. And Miss Toni Rossetti is going to hurt, too. We'll enjoy her before we give her back to her brother. When he's finally agreed a deal."

Dyson looked at Graham.

"Unfasten his ankles," he said, his voice now harsh and impatient.

Graham and Melvyn released the rope and held his ankles to keep him from moving.

"Open his legs."

The two men took a leg each, as if Maudie was a wishbone.

"You're a has-been, Morgan. Out of your class. I almost feel sorry for you."

He stepped forward and kicked Maudie in the crutch. The pain convulsed him, even with his legs being held, and he retched.

"He's yours," Steven said. "But no knives and no broken bones."

Through the nausea, he heard the four leaving. Eric was laughing. It was a light and genteel laugh that would not have been out of place at a Rotarian lunch.

"Right," Graham said. "And now, grandad, the fun starts."

Chapter 20

TONI awoke in confusion in someone else's bed.

"Sorry, love. I didn't know anyone was in here."

An elderly woman in a patterned nylon overall apologised from the doorway, retreated and closed the door.

The confusion went. Toni was at Ruth's and Stuart's. The woman was their cleaner. She was safe.

She relaxed under the covers and reflected on what had happened.

Releasing Paolo from above the back door had been difficult. She had used step ladders, pliers and a heavy claw hammer before the carcase had come loose. Her strength had surprised her, and she had managed to lower the dead watchdog on to the clean white sheet she had laid out as a shroud. She had been determined not to drop him.

She dug a grave near the rhododendrons where he used to enjoy rooting, lay him to rest and covered him. All the time, Gerard slept.

The work was accomplished as if she were taking part in a dream. It was only when she had replaced the tools and completed hosing down the pool of blood that she realised she herself was in a mess.

Her clothes were smeared with soil and blood, and she stripped to her underwear in the garden and put the jeans, sweater and shoes in a dustbin before going upstairs for a shower.

The numbness lasted while she dressed and drove to

Ruth's. She realised she was in a kind of shock when she became aware that she was still hammering on the front door, although Stuart had shouted from the bedroom window that he was coming.

It was seven o'clock and the streets were deserted. The sea air smelled fresh. Beyond the garden wall, she could see a milk float approaching as the door opened.

"Good God, Toni. Get in here."

She was pulled inside. It was a good job the streets had been empty. She still held the gun in her right hand.

Ruth took hold of her, arms protective and guiding, and they went into the kitchen.

They didn't demand explanations but made her comfortable and gave her hot sweet tea to drink. She could feel the numbness draining away and her emotions returning and was frightened that she might lose her grip and break down.

She refused to cry and she refused to forget the recent events. She wanted to remember them in detail and use them to fire her hate.

Stuart was shocked when she briefly told them about Gerard, but he posed no delaying questions. He telephoned Jimmy Doc and asked him to go round to the house to look after the bingo manager.

Only then, when she knew help was on the way, did she tell them everything that had happened.

Ruth held her hand and Stuart sat silent and numb. For him, the story was even more unbelievable because he hadn't known Toni's original reasons for bringing Maudie north from London. But there were no recriminations, only sympathy and concern. Whatever needed doing now, he was there to provide support.

When she had finished, the tiredness lapped in, almost as if it had been waiting for her willpower to weaken.

"You need sleep," Ruth said.

"Can't sleep. Too much to do." She stifled a yawn and

struggled to stifle concern that she knew could turn to panic. "What about Maudie? What will they do?"

"He'll be all right," Stuart said. "They won't hurt him. They said they'd call you. That means they still want to talk business."

"But if they phone and I'm not there . . ."

"They can't phone the house," he said. "The line's out. They'll probably call the club. I'll tell Jimmy Doc. He can take the message. But right now you need to rest."

She allowed herself to be persuaded that everything would be all right, even though she knew it wouldn't, and went to bed.

Despite everything, she fell asleep almost immediately.

And now?

It was one o'clock. The five hours' sleep had left her surprisingly calm. Earlier, in the trauma of dawn, she had foreseen nothing in the future but mutual destruction. She had visualised walking alone into the Dysons' club and shooting them both dead before either being shot herself or arrested for murder.

Maudie, she had told herself, was already as dead as poor Paolo and all that was left was revenge.

Sleep and the cushion of safety had activated hope and reason. The horrors she had wanted to preserve in her memory were already diluted. She got out of bed and prepared for a busy day.

Jimmy Doc told her on the telephone that Gerard had come round in mid-morning. He had been stiff and complained of a severe headache. He remembered nothing of his night outdoors. His last recollecion had been playing poker at the flat of a total stranger who had been both a good loser and a generous host, with an inexhaustible supply of whisky.

Gerard also had a needle mark in his arm.

The bingo manager had started sneezing and the Doc had taken him home and put him to bed. When he had left, he was sleeping again.

"He'll be all right," Jimmy Doc said. "He's had more drugs than Boots the Chemist in his time. His stomach carries a government health warning."

Toni stayed with Stuart and Ruth. To go back home meant she would be cut off without a telephone and to go to the club might indicate eagerness. She felt she still had a façade to maintain.

The Doc called again at two forty-five.

"They want to meet you. You have to phone Steven Dyson within the next half hour." He paused. "They're demanding, not asking. I don't like it, Toni. You'd be a fool to go. Maybe it's time for the police."

"We're long past that, Doc. I'll call you later."

The reason and hope of a few hours before were now evaporating. The sense of fatalism was returning.

Why couldn't she be resolute? A woman of action. Was it normal for emotions to change so quickly? Was it her lack of attitude?

If she was determined to see it through and make it work then it would work. She would be resolute and make the telephone call. She would meet Steven Dyson and make a deal that included Maudie's safety.

And in her handbag she would take the Mauser automatic.

Steven Dyson was blatantly and fraudulently soft spoken and considerate on the telephone.

"I'm so glad you called, Toni. We've been so worried about you."

"I'm fine."

"Good. I hope you're well enough for a meeting to finalise things?"

"When and where?"

"Tonight. Midnight. Riley's."

"No. Somewhere more public."
"You're in no position to make conditions, Toni. The merchandise you want is perishable. It needs careful handling."
"I don't trust you, Steven. Simple as that. Four o'clock. Draper's Coffee Lounge. You know where it is?"
"Of course."
"Four o'clock, then. We'll talk with an audience."

Toni arrived at the coffee lounge, the same one she had introduced Maudie to, at seven minutes past four. Steven Dyson had a table by the window but he wasn't admiring the view. He was watching the door.

He got to his feet at her approach and smiled blandly. She sat and looked out at the holidaymakers who were packing the promenade. They had been driven from the sands by the incoming tide and wandered like refugees, clutching the impedimenta of beach life.

"What would you like?" he asked.

A waitress hovered. Her uniform looked cool and formal in contrast to the hot and dishevelled crowd outside. She ordered a pot of tea because it was served in a silver service. Perhaps it was an idea she could export to America.

"You look terrific, Toni."

She knew she did. She had taken care to look terrific. A linen dress in classic lines and a wide-brimmed straw hat.

"Let's make this as brief as possible," she said. "You pollute the air."

He laughed.

"You didn't always have such an aversion to me. As I recall, you quite . . . enjoyed the physical side of our relationship."

"There never was a relationship. It was business. Enjoyment? I'd rather fuck a frog."

He laughed again, but he wasn't amused.

"You should be nice to me. Polite at least."

She took her time lighting a cigarette.

"Why? I loathe you."

The tea arrived and Dyson maintained his smile while it was served.

When the waitress had gone, Toni said, "Business."

"All right. For some reason I find difficult to understand, you want Morgan back. That's agreeable. In return, we want your brother's signature on a contract of sale." He reached beneath the table for a briefcase that he opened on his knee. He removed a large brown envelope that he handed to her. "The price is now £100,000. Very generous, in the circumstances."

Toni put the envelope on the table without opening it.

"Is Maudie unharmed?"

"Of course. Get the contract signed and you can have him back."

"When?"

"As soon as you like."

"Nine o'clock tonight at the Pleasure Beach. Outside the Fun House, by the laughing clown."

"The laughing clown?"

"He sits in a glass case and laughs."

"The contract?"

"It will be signed."

"Then I'll have Morgan there, and a banker's draft. Don't try anything foolish, Toni. People would only get hurt."

"I'll be there with the contract and I'll be alone. I just want to get this finished."

"Don't we all."

He left without saying goodbye and she remained to drink the tea and envy the holidaymakers beyond the double glazing.

Chapter 21

THEY started with a plastic bag.

It was very effective. With his hands tied behind his back, he could do nothing but suffer and tell himself they had not been given permission to kill him.

The gloves he still wore prompted them to use the bag. They said it would cure him of his kinky desire for rubberwear.

On the first two occasions they placed it over his head, he remained conscious. Even though he knew they would remove it before he suffocated, he could not help but panic. His chest heaved and he sucked desperately and open mouthed against the plastic. They found it amusing. The third time he passed out.

They subsequently used the bag as light relief from beating him. He consoled himself with the thought that while they were suffocating him, they were not damaging him physically.

The two men were systematic and enjoyed their work. But they were amateurs, little boys let loose with a toy. They stripped him of his shirt and used their fists, feet, the baseball bat and a leather cosh. But they never knew how far they could really go in inflicting permanent damage that would not show.

Maudie moaned and cried out at the blows and kicks to make them believe they were more effective than they were. They did not use knives, mark his face or break any limbs. Even so, he suspected they had eventually cracked a rib. At least they didn't pull his fingernails.

Towards the end, when they were tiring and the hurt had built into one continuous ache, he sank into a no-man's-land where time had no meaning. The pain kindled mixed-up memories of long ago.

It became a beating that he was inflicting, one of the many from the past, down the Mile End Road. Then it changed, to a racecourse fight. He was outnumbered and in serious danger until Frankie came. Who was with Frankie? Small, flash dresser and a bloody handful with a razor. Dapper Dan, that was it. But this wasn't Dan or Frankie. Where the hell were they? Where was Ronnie? Jesus, it hurt.

They roused him with a bucket of cold water. He was lying face down on the concrete, his hands and feet untied. It was immaterial. Every breath was painful and immediate retaliation was out of the question.

Hands lifted him and propped him against the wall once more. His head was tilted back and a drink poured down his throat. It burned pleasantly. Whisky?

"Here, grandad. You've been a sport. Have a drink on us."

The bottle was placed in his arms and the two men went away, through the internal door.

Steven Dyson had kept his promise. He hurt severely.

Cradling the whisky bottle, he flexed the fingers of one hand. They worked. He manoeuvred the bottle and tried the other hand. That worked, too.

Slowly, so as not to drop it, he lifted the bottle to his mouth with both hands and drank. Maybe it would ease the pain.

He could hear them laughing through the open door and the sound of a tap running. The dimensions of the warehouse came back into focus.

Why had they given him the whisky?

He peeled off the surgical gloves before taking another drink. He poured more over his shoulders and chest, using it like after shave, wiping it up his arms. He poured it over the crutch of his trousers and down the inside of one thigh.

The bottle was now less than half full. He cradled it in his arms, as they had placed it, and closed his eyes.

His feigned sleep became real and he awoke to the sound of their voices.

"Dirty sod's pissed himself."

Someone kicked his foot. He tensed and opened his eyes.

"Come on, grandad. Time to get dressed."

Graham held Maudie's shirt and jacket.

As they dressed him, he feebly fought to hold on to the whisky bottle. They laughed and when they had finished, Graham took it from him and poured the remains of it over his head.

"Don't worry. There's another," he said. And then, to Melvyn, "Get the van."

Melvyn opened an up-and-under door and walked out into a yard that was enclosed by a high red-brick wall. He climbed into a grey Transit and reversed it until it was alongside Maudie. He climbed out and walked round to open a sliding door in the nearside.

"There you go, grandad." Graham grinned with his white even teeth. "A free ride home to the Smoke."

They picked him up by the arms and he groaned and rolled his eyes. They pushed him inside and propped him up alongside the open door.

"What did I say?" That bloody grin again. "Something to drink on the way."

He took the top off another bottle and pushed it into his arms.

The sliding door shut and for a few seconds he was alone. He tipped some of the scotch on to his jacket. He could sense that his pockets were empty. Wallet, keys, handkerchief. Nothing in his trouser pockets either, and they had taken his watch before the beating started. He was unidentifiable. An inebriate dosser.

Melvyn climbed back into the driving seat, started the engine and drove into the yard. The warehouse door rattled shut and Graham got into the passenger seat. They set off.

He moaned when they went over bumps and slumped to one side when they went round a corner, although he struggled to keep the bottle straight.

Graham leaned over from the front to push him upright again.

"That's it, grandad. Don't spill it."

He took a noisy drink and both men laughed.

Before long the road straightened and they picked up speed. There were no more bumps. They had reached the motorway. The M56, the Sunshine Highway.

He poured away more of the scotch, on to the floor of the van, and took more noisy swigs. He moved the position of his legs, raising his left knee so that he could rest his head upon it. He could feel Graham watching him.

He dropped the bottle and let it roll away. His breathing was deep and laboured and he made no attempt to move.

"Silly old sod's asleep," Graham said.

The fingers of his right hand rested against the sole of his left shoe. At least they hadn't pulled his fingernails.

Ten, fifteen minutes. A change of speed.

"Outside lane. Stay right," Graham instructed. "Two or three miles and there's a long downhill. It belts along."

The van leaned into a long gradual bend, levelled, and the sound of traffic increased. There were heavy wagons, now, as well as family saloons. They accelerated. They had joined the M6, the main arterial route through the north-west. Blackpool was a resort well served by motorways, he had noted from the maps. Good for getaways. Good for accidents.

Graham climbed into the back and shook his shoulder.

"Wake up, grandad. Nearly there."

Maudie raised his head as if with great effort and squinted at the even teeth.

"Silly old sod. Coming all this way and thinking you could still do the business. Just you and a bunch of hairy-arsed Jocks." He shook his head.

The van picked up more speed as it started downhill.

The fair-haired thug crouched alongside Maudie and slid open the van's side door. The air was warm with both summer and fumes.

It was beaten into shapes of sound as different vehicles were overtaken. Soft and smooth for a car, heavy and menacing for a lorry.

Graham retrieved the whisky bottle and balanced himself behind the seats to look over Melvyn's shoulder at the traffic ahead.

"The cement truck. Hold position in front of it."

He turned back to Maudie who still squinted, helpless and bemused.

"You don't want to go without your bottle, do you?"

He leaned forward, pushed it into Maudie's jacket pocket, and took hold of Maudie's lapels with both hands.

"Bye, bye, grandad."

He still grinned.

Maudie raised his right hand feebly, almost as if he intended to wave, and wiped it quickly across the man's forehead.

"Ready!" shouted Melvyn from the driver's seat.

"For fuck's sake . . . ?"

Graham's voice changed from quizzical to sudden awareness as the blood spurted into his eyes. His mouth fell open slackly, the grin gone, and he released the lapels to put his hands to his face.

"Tommo! Ready!" urged Melvyn.

The cement truck thundered outside the door.

Maudie braced his back against the side of the van, lowered his left knee and kicked hard with his right leg. His foot connected fiercely with Graham's testicles and the young thug's balance tipped forward. Maudie aided his shift in equilibrium by pulling his tie and pushing his left shoulder.

He went head first through the door without a sound.

"Fucking hell!" said Melvyn.

The van veered. Melvyn looked over his shoulder, his face white. He steered one handed and fumbled in a pocket with the other.

Maudie gathered his strength and rolled across the van until he was behind the driver's seat. He pulled himself to his knees, holding on to Melvyn's shoulder with his left hand. His right hand held the bloodstained half of the razor blade that had been hidden beneath the sole of his shoe. He lowered it in front of Melvyn's face until it rested against his throat.

Thank God they hadn't pulled his fingernails.

"Watch the road, son," he said. "We don't want an accident."

Maudie directed him to take the next available slip road off the motorway. It was a large clover leaf at the bottom of the hill. Melvyn cut across a Cortina estate in the middle lane but made it. They went all the way round the leaf and rejoined the motorway to drive back along the northbound carriageway.

Halfway up the hill, vehicles had stopped in ungainly shunts. The cement truck was nose first on the hard shoulder with its rear blocking the nearside lane. A van was stuck beneath its tailgate. The middle lane was also blocked, and cars, coaches and lorries filtered past in the outside lane.

Maudie guessed that about all that would be left of Graham would be his Stanley knife and those even white teeth.

Self-preservation and bloody mindedness had given him the strength to achieve the first part, and adrenalin had taken him across the van to hold the blade at Melvyn's throat. But he needed a rest. He ached, his ribs hurt, and every time he breathed he inhaled needles. The whisky was also having an effect and making him tired.

"What's in your pocket?"

"What?"

"You were reaching for something. What is it?"

He hesitated, but only for a moment.

"A shooter."

"You amaze me. That's a big boy's toy." He scraped bristle with the blade. "The jugular will give the windscreen an instant respray. You won't be able to see out. You'll crash. But you won't care. You'll be dead." He paused. "Now. Very slowly. Take the gun out of your pocket. Two fingers only. And pass it to me."

Melvyn obeyed.

It was a Luger automatic. The same model German officers had used in the First World War.

"Gordon Bennett. This came out of the ark. Does Anton Diffring know you've got it?"

"Who?"

"Never mind."

He removed the blade from Melvyn's throat and sat back on the floor of the van. It was an ideal position from which to maintain command. If the driver annoyed him he could shoot him through the seat. He could also, for the first time, relax. Melvyn would take no chances with an unseen threat.

"What time is it?"

"Half past seven."

"How's Dyson going to get Toni Rossetti?"

"I don't know."

"Look. Let's not piss about. I can start with your kneecaps. I don't give a shit."

"A meeting. He was arranging a meeting but I don't know where or when. Maybe tonight. He phoned this afternoon to tell us to get rid of you. Tommo – Graham –

said he sounded pleased with himself. So it's maybe tonight."

Maudie tried to think things out but the pain wouldn't let him.

"Who's at the warehouse?"

"Nobody."

"If there is, you're the first I shoot."

"There's nobody there."

"Then go to the warehouse."

Chapter 22

TONI went to the house to collect her thoughts and clothes for the meeting that was planned for that night.

Julian, the Barnsley bouncer, and Mrs Bradshaw were both there to give the place an air of normality she felt it didn't deserve. The only indication that anything had happened the night before was that the telephone was still out of order.

Ruth arrived at six o'clock.

"I got worried," she said. "I thought you might be here."

"I needed some time on my own. I'm all right."

"How was Dyson? Slimy as ever?"

"Slimier. We came to an agreement."

Ruth pursed her lips.

"Will it work?"

"It has to work. We've come to the end of the line. We both know that. Next stop is murder."

"So what's the agreement?"

"They've made an offer that's halfway to being reasonable, plus Maudie is delivered back in one piece. We sign the contracts tomorrow. It's now in the hands of solicitors," she lied. "All safe and sanitised. Nobody else gets hurt."

Ruth stared as if she didn't believe her.

"Are you telling me the truth?"

Toni gave her a tired smile.

"I'm beat, Ruth. It's all over."

Her friend embraced her sadly and sighed.

"They're bastards and I hate what they've done. Please God somebody will pay them back, some time. But, in one
sense, I'm glad it's over. I was getting really scared." She broke away. "Have you seen the *Gazette*?"

"No. Why?"

Ruth pulled the evening newspaper from her large shoulder bag and handed it over. The headline on the front page read:

MURDER HUNT AFTER
GANG FIGHT DEATH

Toni took the paper and read the opening paragraphs:

"Blackpool police today launched a murder hunt after a 19-year-old Scottish youth died following a gang fight.

"Three other youths are still in Victoria Hospital – one in intensive care – suffering from knife wounds and multiple injuries.

"All are believed to be from Stirling.

"They were found on a car park near Talbot Road Bus Station in the early hours of Sunday morning after a taxi driver called the police . . . "

She scanned the rest but there was no mention of the disturbance in the Life of Riley that happened on the same night.

Ruth said, "It's the Dysons, isn't it? The lads Jimmy Doc told you about. They are really nasty people. Thank God you're out of it. No matter what. At least you're getting out in one piece."

Ruth was now a complication that Toni needed to distance from danger. Her plan was simple.

She suggested they go into town for an early meal and Ruth talked to Mrs Bradshaw in the living room while Toni got ready.

At seven o'clock she shouted for her friend from the hall and they went out to the parked cars. Toni climbed into the driving seat of the Mercedes and Ruth looked ready to argue.

"It would be easier if we took mine," she said. "Easier to park and you won't have to count your drinks."

"You take yours, Ruth. I'll take mine."

"What?"

Ruth stepped closer to the car and reached out to the door handle.

"They're locked." The electric window slid up until there was only a two-inch gap. "I'm sorry, Ruth. That meeting I told you about is tonight. I have to do it on my own. Don't worry. And don't try to follow me." Toni smiled. "You can't. I took your car keys. They're in a drawer in my bedroom. By the time you find them I'll be gone."

"Toni, no. Think things out. Let me get Stuart."

"I have thought things out. Everything's going to be all right. And you can help, if you want. Go home and sit by the phone. I'll need you when it's over. I'll call you. And we'll head for the nearest bar."

Toni put the car into gear and drove out of the gate and on to the main road. In the rear-view mirror, she saw that Ruth had remained standing on the gravel, staring after her.

Good. She would not be pursued. She would have time to park the car and prepare herself with a walk on the Promenade.

She had time to kill. Then, at the Pleasure Beach, she might have something else to kill.

Chapter 23

THERE was a problem at the warehouse. The door was closed, which meant one of them had to get out to open it.

"Park the van so I can watch you through the side door," Maudie instructed.

Melvyn did as he was told and then slid open the driver's door to get out.

"Don't be stupid," Maudie said. "Climb over. You're going out, and getting back in, this way."

Maudie kept the gun trained on him throughout the operation. Finally, they were inside, the door closed again.

"Well done. I think we've found something you're good at. You should be a doorman."

Maudie eased himself out of the van. His legs were unsteady and he leaned against the side of the vehicle for support. The baseball bat that they had used earlier was propped against the folding chair.

"Get me the bat. Carefully."

The youth looked at the bat and glanced back at Maudie before he went for it. Maudie saw the look in his eyes. The stupid bastard thought he had a chance. Well. It was marginally better than no chance at all.

Melvyn picked up the bat in his right hand by the handle. Maudie didn't correct him. He was tired and wanted events to speed up. Let him have his seconds of hope.

He approached, the bat held out to one side, innocuous but ready to swing. Maudie allowed him to get as close as six feet before he shot him. Twice. Two chest shots. They echoed in the empty warehouse.

Melvyn stopped as if someone had slammed a door in his face. He took a step backwards and looked down at his chest. The baseball bat fell to the floor. It clattered and rolled across the uneven concrete. He tried to raise his head to look at Maudie but it kept on going back and he fell the same way, arms and legs spread like a pinned specimen.

Maudie picked up the bat and used it as a walking stick. He paused by the body and the staring eyes confirmed that Melvyn was dead. He felt no remorse. He felt nothing. The past had taught him to subdue emotions because they got in the way. Besides, he ached too much to give a toss.

He walked, painfully, to the inner door. It led into an office with a desk, two chairs and a telephone. Another door led outside.

He eased himself into the seat at the desk. It had a patchwork cushion on it. He pulled the telephone towards him and found a directory in a desk drawer. He tried the house but the line was out of order.

He rang the club and someone he didn't know told him that neither Jimmy Doc nor Toni Rossetti was there. Jimmy Doc was not expected until nine thirty.

Ruth Shapiro. She might be at Ruth's. There were three Shapiro's in the directory but only one Stuart. Ruth answered.

"It's Morgan. Is Toni there?"

"Maudie! Are you all right?"

"I'm okay. Is Toni there?"

"No. She's gone to meet Steven Dyson. She thought . . . we thought . . . "

"I know. Well, they don't have me any more. Did she say where she was going?"

"No. Stuart's out looking for her."

"Or what time she was meeting him?"

"Only that it was some time tonight. She tricked me. She wanted to go alone. I tried . . . "

"Never mind, Ruth. Listen. You have to come and get me. Now." He gave her the name of the road where the warehouse was located. "I'll be outside. And be quick. She's in danger."

After he replaced the receiver in its cradle, he allowed himself a moment's rest. He gazed round the office and realised he had some tidying up to do.

His wallet, minus money, and watch were in a desk drawer. He pocketed them. There was no sign of the razor. In all probability, it was lying somewhere in the garden at the house near where he had been coshed.

Then, with a cloth, he cleaned up any surface he might have touched. He had been careful, with this in mind, and had left few traces. But he took no chances with the whisky bottles, which he had handled extensively. He found the empty one in a waste bin in the warehouse and put it, together with the one from the van, into one of the clear plastic bags they had used over his head.

When he was satisfied, he let himself out and leaned against the yard gate, still using the baseball bat as a walking stick, and waited for Ruth.

The warehouse was located a couple of miles inland and the road was quiet. Opposite was a row of shops that were all closed. Further along were a school and terraced houses with neatly walled front gardens. He was out of place. It was the wrong area for drunks and derelicts.

Ruth arrived with a screech of brakes. A bleeding sports car. A bleeding red sports car.

She pushed open the nearside door for him and then, when she saw his state, got out and ran round to help him.

"Jesus Christ. What happened?"

"The Dysons happened." He winced as he fed a leg into the car. "Did Toni give you any clue where she might be?"

"No. But she told me to stay by the phone. She said

she'd call me after it was all over. Stuart's looking for her. Going to places she might be, driving round looking for her car."

Ruth slid behind the wheel and wrinkled her nose at his smell.

"The safe house," he said. "Take me to the safe house. And be quick."

The journey did not take long. On the way, Ruth talked non stop. She was naturally garrulous and the excitement had hyped her up. She speculated about where Toni might be and how earlier she had thought everything was settled.

"I was so relieved. Especially after reading about the murder hunt."

"Murder hunt?"

"A Scottish lad. Nineteen. They said it was a gang fight. The others are in hospital. The lads from Stirling that Jimmy Doc told you about, who got thrown out of Riley's. When I first heard about it, I thought they were relatives of the Doc's. They're not related are they, Maudie?"

"They're not related. They're just unlucky."

At the house he told her where the spare key was hidden in the garden and she unlocked the front door and helped him inside.

"You stink."

"Can't be helped. There isn't time for a bath."

He winced again and held his side.

"What is it?"

"Busted rib, I think. There's tape upstairs. You'll have to tape me."

"Where is it?"

"In the suitcase on top of the wardrobe. Bring the case down."

He took off the jacket and ripped open the shirt whilst

she went upstairs. By the time she returned he was stripped to the waist.

"My God. What a mess."

"I look better when I breathe in."

"What did they hit you with?"

"Anything they had. Look. Stop admiring it and tape it."

She placed the suitcase on the coffee table and dropped clean clothes in a chair.

"You can at least change. You stink to high heaven and . . . "

He opened the suitcase and she was silenced by its contents. He handed her a wide roll of surgical tape.

"Tape me."

She still looked at the open suitcase.

"Are you going to start a war?"

"No. I'm going to finish one. Tape me."

She taped him from his waist to his armpits, encasing him tightly in the strong self adhesive.

"Save some for my leg."

He allowed her to remove his trousers without embarrassment and pointed out where he wanted the tape around his left thigh. When she had finished she helped him to dress in slacks and knitted shirt.

"What time is it?"

He leaned against the back of an armchair and pretended he felt better.

"Half eight."

"Get the hire car out of the garage. The keys are under the driver's seat. I'll follow you."

Ruth hesitated.

"What is it?" he said.

"Why not call the police?"

"No time. They'd ask questions before they'd do anything. And it's too late. There's no way to stop this now. All you can do is ride it out."

She nodded, although he knew she did not fully understand, and went out of the back door.

Maudie pulled on a lightweight trenchcoat that was hanging in the hall. It was too stylish for his age but perfect for his purpose.

The pockets were merely slits. He could put his hands through and scratch his bollocks if he wanted to. Below the slits, on the inside, were patch pockets. He put on a fresh pair of surgical gloves that he took from the suitcase before he began.

In the left-hand pocket he put three canisters, two of smoke and one of CS gas. He wiped the Luger of prints and stuck it into his belt, the butt concealed by the loose shirt. The flick knife with the six-inch blade he taped horizontally on to the tape that covered his stomach. He did it with care so that it would tug loose if he needed it.

He picked up the shotgun and felt its power. It was a beauty. An Ithica stakeout gun. They had a wicked way with weapons in the United States.

A five-shot, slide-action repeater with short barrel and pistol grip. It was fully loaded and he put a handful of extra 20-gauge cartridges into the right-hand patch pocket.

He put his hand through the slit pocket and took hold of the grip. The gun lay beneath the folds of the coat, ready and lethal.

Ready to go the limit.

Chapter 24

THERE was almost an hour to kill. That phrase again. As if time was an enemy. It was.

She had spent the best part of her life killing time, staying busy to avoid the emptiness. The only period in her life when time was an ally was childhood, when she had looked forward to birthdays or Christmas.

Even then it was fickle, passing slowly before the event and speeding up when it arrived. It was as if good times were either anticipated or remembered, but never actually experienced.

Time warped reality. What had happened in the past weeks, last night even, was memories. It was only real while it happened, while the fear or excitement could be tasted.

Now she was in limbo again, reliant, as ever, upon time. There was no anticipation, no quickening of the senses. There was an hour to kill before reality returned.

She parked the car in a side street near the Promenade and walked on to the front. The air had a chill that was more noticeable because the day had been so hot. Heavy clouds filled the horizon over the Irish Sea with the threat of a summer storm.

She wore the same dress she had worn for the coffee-room meeting with Steven Dyson a few hours before, but now wore a tan Jaeger cardigan with it, and leather gloves, and had swopped the high heels for flat shoes. The large raffia bag on her shoulder contained the brown envelope he had given her.

Families wandered the Promenade, past the arcades, cafes and pubs, faces glowing from a day on the beach. Those without kids were in the bars, spending their holiday money and getting louder by the minute.

A photographer bumped into her as she hesitated outside the Sleaze Bar, grinned an apology, and went in, bag on shoulder, camera in one hand and tickets in the other.

A smudger. It was a good name. Few had ever had any training so their results were unlikely to win awards. And if their pictures were out of focus, so what? The punters were usually out of focus, too.

They captured smiling, drunken faces by the thousand, immortalising small slices of holiday. The punters treasured their six by fours. The pictures proved they had had a good time. She walked on.

The sights, sounds and smells were dominated by frying onions and fish and chips. At times, where the quick-snack joints lapped each other's counters, the pavement was carpeted with half filled polystyrene trays. The revolting debris of fast food.

Outside a fancy goods shop she swung a rack of cartoon postcards. Fat women, small men in bowler hats and moustaches, busty blondes showing stocking tops. They had hardly changed in thirty years.

At a nearby stall three girls were choosing silly hats. They squealed with laughter as they tried them on and made fun of each other in Yorkshire accents.

Toni had forgotten how northern accents varied so much. When her father had been alive he had always had a calendar that listed the textile holiday dates of the cotton towns of Lancashire and the woollen towns of Yorkshire. Week by week the accents had changed. Accrington different from Blackburn, Huddersfield different from Bradford.

Their residents were still coming here on holiday, even though textiles was no longer king. The girls had probably saved their giros for a week of escape.

"Ooh, that's a right belter, Michelle. Look. Look, our Debbie. Intit? Intit a right belter?"

"It's a bit mucky, though. I mean. Lads'll think you're a right fast cat."

"Well they won't be far wrong, will they? Do owt for a chocolate biscuit, won't you, chuck?"

Toni laughed with them, envied them. The only complications they had tonight were finding three young men and then finding their way back to the boarding house through the alcohol.

She went into one of the many cafes and bought an espresso coffee. The gurgles of the machine reminded her of the sixties, black and white mini dresses, pep pills and northern soul at the Twisted Wheel.

One of the disc jockeys had been keen on her. A lean and good-looking bloke with a mind as sharp as his clothes. He'd gone on to make a fortune in hairdressing in London.

Perhaps she should have married him, settled down, had kids before the trouble with her first husband had come along. But the future had been too enticing. All those possibilities for a single girl . . .

She had forever remained a single girl, despite two marriages. A wedding certificate didn't change your life. Kids changed your life. So here she was, still single, still chasing.

It might all have been different if. Always if. If she hadn't married her first husband was a good one to start with.

She should have insisted they married during the season. If she had, he might not have turned up. If she had, no one would have turned up, including the family. The season dominated life.

Blackpool people took holidays out of season, decorated their houses and businesses, socialised and had parties out of season. Her father had died out of season. So she had dutifully waited until early November to be married, after the holidaymakers had gone.

He had been a hotelier and she had said yes to spite a friend. That hadn't been the only reason but it had been a contributory factor. It didn't last long after she discovered his violent temper. He was a lovely man until provoked and, she had to admit, she had been good at provoking him. One hiding too many made her walk out. Divorce and another wedding followed.

Only then did she discover the legacy of her first marriage. A punch in the stomach had damaged fallopian tubes that no amount of fertility treatment would put right. She would never have children.

Without a child she saw no reason to remain with her second husband. She divorced again.

But if she had married the disc jockey . . . ?

When she rejected him, he left town. If she had said yes, he might now be blaming her for lost opportunities.

She drank the coffee.

If she had said yes. Would reality have been better than the dreams? They could now be living in St Annes with two kids, a dog and a seasonal business that gave them the winter to themselves. They might have been very happy. She would have been very happy.

The smudger she had seen earlier came in, grinned at her in recognition when their eyes met, and went to the self-service counter.

Paranoia came knocking. What was he doing here? Was he following her? Was he one of Dyson's mob?

She forced herself to calm down. Smudgers worked hard, long hours, like everyone else in the season. Like everyone else, they needed a break, now and then.

He came towards her. The camera was hanging on its strap around his neck and he carried a coffee.

"Anybody sitting here?"

"No."

"Do you mind?"

"Not at all."

He sat down and put his bag on the floor. He was in his late twenties, quick eyed and personable. A charmer rather than a looker, the sort whose personality made you forget that the nose was slightly too big and the mouth too mobile.

Wrong time, wrong place. Otherwise . . .

"The name's Dave." He poured sugar into his coffee. "You're not on holiday. Local?"

"Sort of."

"Sort of. Intriguing." He sipped the coffee. "I'm sort of, too. From Bolton, but the perks are better here." He winked.

She smiled but didn't reply.

"How come you're on your own? Meeting someone?"

"Eventually."

"Not me?"

"No."

He pulled a face.

"Shame. Still, I'm on duty anyway." He looked towards the counter. "Grabbing a bite before it gets busy. It'll be bloody murder later." He touched the camera. "I take snaps." He grinned. "I could give you a special rate."

"I'm sure you could."

"I don't suppose there's any point in asking for your phone number?"

Her smile broadened. She was right. He was better looking already.

"Why don't you give me yours?" she said.

"Eh?" His eyes widened, then he grinned. "With pleasure." He took a business card from his top pocket. "I'm usually in until twelve. Mornings. You probably won't call but I can dream. And in case it helps, let me stress that I'm very clean, have all my own teeth and know a very reasonable Chinese. He's also very clean and has all his own teeth."

She laughed.

"I'll bear it in mind."

A bored youth in chef's uniform shouted from the counter.

"Bacon and egg sandwich."

"Here." Dave raised his arm and the youth brought it across. "It's not a growler is it, Liam? The last one I had got me by the throat."

"This one's tenderised. Personal. I've been kicking it up and down behind the range for two hours. Washed my boots first."

"Everybody in this town's a comedian." He shook his head. "You'd better hurry or you'll miss the second house at the North Pier."

Liam walked back to the counter and Toni watched his boots. She could imagine he did kick the bacon about. It would relieve the boredom and repay the rudeness. She wondered how many rashers of growler bacon he had handy for drunks and loudmouths. It paid to be polite.

"Mm." Dave lifted the top off the sandwich and looked inside. He put salt on the contents and replaced it. "If you were thinking of going, now would be a good time."

"I beg your pardon?"

"I'm thinking of my image. These are messy buggers. One mouthful, wrong pressure in the wrong place, the yolk goes ape and I ruin a beautiful friendship, not to mention your cardy."

Toni laughed and picked up her bag.

"It's a long time since I've been sweet talked so effectively." She got up. "I was going anyway."

"Don't forget to call."

"I just might. Have a nice night."

Chapter 25

THEY drove past Riley's and Maudie noted the dress-suited security out front. He directed Ruth into the side street, where the entrances to the office extension and the staff car park were located

"Turn the car round and park further down the street so you can watch for me coming out. Don't leave the engine running and don't rev it when you start up again. When we drive away, drive normally. Signal at the end of the road and turn right, away from the club. Okay?"

"Okay."

He hesitated and then reached across with his left hand to squeeze her arm.

"I didn't want you to get involved. There was nobody else."

"Is Toni in there?"

"I don't know. I don't think so. I don't think they would be dumb enough to bring her here. I don't know if she's met them yet, but someone will know where she is and I'll make them tell me."

She nodded.

"I'll be ready. I'll do as you say."

"Good girl."

Getting out of the car was painful but once he was on his feet it wasn't too bad. Anyway, he would forget the aggravation when the action started.

He went first to the office door but it was locked as he had expected. It had a security peephole and he knew the number of locks holding it. It was one to forget going in. Maybe one to remember coming out.

There were three vehicles in the staff car park. A Rover limousine with current registration, a Cortina and an Escort, both a few years old. The Rover was obviously management, the others staff.

Keeping the cars between himself and the rear door, he went to the Rover and crouched behind it. His legs gave way and he fell to his knees. He steadied himself with his left hand and made sure the shotgun didn't touch the ground. He looked towards the building. The door was flanked by waste bins as big as a man, and steam came from an extractor fan high in the wall above them.

He let the air out of one of the Rover's front tyres. Simple precaution in case he had to pursue or was pursued. Then, before he moved on, he had a sudden thought. He found a sharp stone on the ground and scrawled a single word along the side of the limo's paintwork.

One window in the extension overlooked the car park but no one was there. He got up and walked to the door. It opened outwards and was not locked. From within came kitchen smells. He pulled it open and stepped inside, into a small room containing mops, buckets, a dustbin and a stack of toilet rolls.

An inner door was open and led into the kitchen. Somebody was shouting at somebody else and a pan clattered but there was little activity. Too early for meals. Not too early for music. He could hear muffled disco sounds.

He stepped into the doorway and assessed the place. A large serving hatch to the left was, at the moment, shuttered. Griddle, grills and range to his left, a central preparation table and a door to the right.

Two men in kitchen whites were at the far side of the preparation table. They both turned to stare. He stared back.

"Can I help you?"

The fat one spoke and he asked the question in a tone that was half belligerent.

"I'm here to see Mr Dyson."

"Well you've come a funny way."

"Where is he?"

"You should have used the front door.

"Where is he?"

"Is he expecting you?"

Maudie raised the shotgun from the folds of the coat. He allowed them a second to realise exactly what it was.

"Where is he?"

Both men developed slack jaws. The fat one took a hesitant step back. This time, the thin one spoke.

"Mr Eric's upstairs."

Maudie headed for the door. Alongside it on the wall was a telephone. He ripped the handset from its wire, replaced it, then went through the door, lowering the gun back beneath the coat.

He was in the fun bar. Near the ladies'. It was a large room that was mostly filled with tables, raised crescent alcoves on the far side, a stage beyond the shuttered food bar to his left. There was a dance floor in front of the stage. The bars ran along the wall to his right, past the ladies'.

The corner into which he had emerged was dimly lit. The rest of the room was alive with changing lights. The disco music was louder than he had expected. There were plenty of customers, even though it was still early for a late-hours night spot, and they were all young and hyper active. They laughed and gesticulated and conducted conversations at a shout. Maudie was glad he was old.

The front entrance was at the other end of the room, to his right. Two large penguins were this side of the foyer. They were operating a double or possibly triple vetting process as people came in.

He allowed his eyes to get accustomed to the lights. The

music was beginning to hurt his ears. It was a pound to a penny the stairs were in the foyer.

He reached into his pocket and took out a canister. The door of the ladies' swung open and two girls came out giggling. Perhaps giggling was compulsory. All the girls seemed to be doing it.

They didn't notice him and departed into the throng but the light from the lavatory allowed him to check the sort of canister he held, before he stepped back into the kitchen.

The two men were at the far end of the room. They hadn't moved, but they had been whispering urgently together. His re-entrance silenced them and they looked round sharply.

"Open the serving hatches," he ordered.

They looked at each other and scurried to obey. The disco noise invaded the room and the lights made psychedelic patterns on their faces.

"You've never seen me," he said. "Have you?"

They shook their heads.

Maudie ripped the pin from the canister and threw it on to the preparation table.

"Fire bomb," he said. He pointed the gun at the hatches. "Time to evacuate."

They went through the hatches. The thin one went first and fell out of the other side in his eagerness.

"Fire! Get out. Fire," he shouted, as he scrambled to his feet.

The fat one followed, saying nothing, concentrating on getting his bulk through the narrow space. The smoke billowed around him.

Maudie went back through the door into the bar. People near the hatches were staring at the two chefs and the smoke. Those further back in the room had so far noticed nothing.

The thin man pushed through the tables shouting fire, heading for the front foyer. The smoke was thickening now and the fat man was trying to follow but the closest punters were finally getting to their feet and hampering his escape. He began screaming.

It amazed Maudie how slowly people reacted. They preferred to look. He walked along the side of the room, past the ladies', to the drinkers near the bar.

"Fire in the kitchens. Everybody out," he told them. To the staff behind the bars, he said, "Fire in the kitchen. Get everybody out. It's spreading fast."

He moved on quickly to avoid getting caught in the gathering panic. The bouncers by the foyer had moved deeper into the room to see what was happening and he glanced back.

The smoke was white and thick near the kitchen. People were pushing, trying to get away, knocking over tables and chairs and smashing glasses.

Maudie stepped behind the bouncers and went through the swing glass doors into the foyer. Two more men in dress suits looked at him. One was standing by the door, the other sitting behind a cash desk. Beyond the desk was a flight of stairs.

"The place is on fire," he said. "Call the fire brigade."

There was no reaction.

He levelled the shotgun from beneath his coat. This time, reaction was swift.

The bouncer by the door went through it in a dive, the one behind the desk raised his hands.

"Take it. It's not my money. No trouble. Just take it."

"Where's Dyson?"

"Upstairs. In his office."

"Where?"

"Top of the stairs."

He walked past the cash desk and up the stairs. The climb was painful and he paused to get his breath two steps from the top. A door four feet away opened and Paul Unsworth stepped through it. The dickie suit was expensive. The penguins went to Burton's but he was made to measure by the best.

Unsworth stopped in shock and his eyes widened. It was the split second that was the difference between survival and death. If he had reacted immediately, he might have made it back through the door. But he didn't.

Maudie raised the shotgun into the cradle of his left hand, fired, and pumped the next cartridge into the chamber.

The elegant hardman went backwards as if plucked by a stunt wire. His feet never touched as he hit the jamb of the door he had just left, and flopped into the corridor. His white shirt was a total mess.

Maudie took the last two steps and went down the corridor to the open door. One pace inside, one pace sideways. His back was against the wall, the gun covered the room.

Eric Dyson sat behind a leather-topped desk. The cigar dropped out of his mouth and continued to burn on his blotter. Everyone, it appeared to Maudie, was in slow motion.

"Where's Toni?"

"How . . . how . . . ?"

He was so shaken he was blubbering. Maudie stepped closer, picked up the cigar with his left hand and stubbed it out on Dyson's forehead.

The man screamed, his plump hands flopping ineffectually. But the pain brought his senses back.

Maudie placed the barrel of the shotgun against his cheek.

"Where is she?"

"She's not here."

He clubbed him with the barrel.

"Where?"

"Steven's meeting her outside the Fun House at the Pleasure Beach. Nine o'clock."

Maudie moved the barrel until it pointed straight at his face.

"It's the truth. She chose the place."

He was close to blubbing again.

Maudie backed off towards the door. He was running out of time.

"Where will he take her?"

"The warehouse. To meet Mel and Graham."

He was sniffling to hold back tears. His nose was running and he was too frightened to contemplate wiping it. It was a long time since Maudie had seen anyone so frightened. It was a mercy, in a way, to pull the trigger.

A head shot wiped away the snot and did not leave a great deal else to identify. It was a necessary execution and that was justification enough.

Security had finally woken up. Two of them were coming up the stairs. At the sight of the gun they froze in mid-step. Behind them, the foyer was full of customers pushing to get out. They were wet. The smoke must have activated a sprinkler system.

He fired a shot into the ceiling and the duo fell flat. The plaster dusted their shoulders like heavy dandruff.

He went along the corridor, taking out another canister, pulling the pin and dropping it behind him to discourage pursuit. He turned a corner and was confronted by a locked door.

It was new and it was about the right place for a connecting door into the extension. He fired into the lock. The door jumped and sagged but held at the top of the frame. He fired again at the point of resistance and the remains bounced open.

It did lead into the extension and a few yards along was the door into the conference room and Steven's suite. Beyond it were the stairs. Going down, his left leg gave way and he fell against the banister.

He knew the outer door at the bottom was double

locked. It also opened inwards and shooting it open might be difficult. He went into the office.

A frosted glass window overlooked the street. It was fitted with a safety lock that he couldn't release. He put the shotgun down on a desk and gripped a chair. Picking it up hurt his ribs and made him wince. He didn't swing it, but rammed the legs into the pane, and the glass shattered outwards.

He dropped the chair, picked up the shotgun and ran its barrel along the bottom of the frame to clear the shards. It was still messy. He placed the chair beneath the window so he could step out and avoid the broken pieces of glass. It meant he didn't cut himself but it gave him a longer drop to the pavement. His left leg gave way again when he landed.

The car pulled up alongside him and he got in.

"Remember. Be normal," he said, massaging his thigh.

He noticed her hands were shaking slightly on the wheel but she signalled right and paused at the junction before pulling into the main road and driving away.

"The Pleasure Beach," he said. She turned a corner and began to speed up. "What time is it?"

"Five to nine."

"You'd better move it."

Chapter 26

THE meeting with the photographer had given her an unnatural high. She had to restrain herself from laughing as she left the coffee bar. In doing so, she became aware that her emotions were on a roller coaster. The Pleasure Beach was an appropriate rendezvous.

She continued along the promenade towards Europe's biggest funfair. Everything in this town had to be the biggest and best. The illuminations were The Greatest Free Show on Earth, the beach was Eight Miles of Golden Sands. This was a resort with three piers, rather than one, and a copy of the Eiffel Tower on its seafront.

It was a town built with brash kiss-me-quick showmanship. Was it any wonder it had failed to prepare her for the rest of her life?

Her emotions were faulty. Stress had taken its toll. She was no longer thinking logically. The last half hour she had indulged in the sort of retrospection a condemned man might be expected to wallow in. It served no purpose, especially as she was not condemned. She should be planning what she was going to do, but the truth was she didn't know. It was a truth from which she had been trying to hide.

Certain events had been set in motion. They could develop in different ways. She was part of them and, hopefully, would be able to influence their course.

Since the previous night she had gone from fatalism to aggression to bland optimism and back. What she had to do now was bottle the confusion. At the Pleasure Beach she had to be decisive.

The envelope containing Steven Dyson's contract was noticeable in her bag. She had forged her brother's signature upon it. That was the price Steven had set for Maudie's freedom. If he reneged, she had the weapon.

She didn't know if the exchange would work or if Steven Dyson intended to go through with it. But it was all she had and she had to make something work. In the final analysis, she would at least settle part of the score.

Now that she had re-routed her thoughts the anger was returning and pushing the feeling of helplessness to one side. The anger was directed at one man, Steven Dyson. It was easier to handle that way.

Make him the culprit, place the total responsibility for everything upon him – her brother's injuries, Emilio's exile, Maudie's pain and her own suffering.

Toni entered the Pleasure Beach at eight forty-five but did not go straight to the Fun House. She mingled with the wandering crowds and used their anonymity for cover.

From different vantage points she viewed the meeting ground. Steven wasn't there yet. She also looked for Dyson associates, but what would they look like? They would hardly be wearing evening suits and carrying iron bars.

A group of people gathered to listen to a spieler pull punters for a bingo game. She joined them.

"Where you from, love?"

"Dublin," said a young woman.

"Blimey. No wonder you're late. Here, take a seat and have a rest. It's a long walk back.

The laughter surrounded her.

"And you, love. Where are you from?"

"Aberystwyth."

"Aberystwyth! Wales! The land of song and sheep. Here! Did you hear about the Welsh sex shop? It sold blow-up sheep."

More laughter.

"No offence, no offence. Come on now, take a seat, the next game's about to start. We give away fun as well as prizes here."

Toni moved on. She climbed a tower that led to the chair lifts that made slow traverses across the funfair from high wires. A window halfway up the tower gave her a clear view of the Fun House.

The clouds had closed in from the sea and the lights below her shone brighter in the unseasonal darkness. The crowds were thinning as the storm got closer, with parents taking their children home to guest-house family rooms.

At exactly nine o'clock Steven Dyson came into sight below her, walking past the mechanical camel races and games of chance. He went up the slope and stopped in front of the glass case that held the laughing clown.

He was alone. A slim young man in dark slacks and a sweater, looking for his date. The clown rolled with laughter and Dyson waited, arms folded, and scanned the groups of people that approached and passed.

He seemed relaxed, at ease. She could see no one nearby who looked like a threat. She could see no sign of Maudie. Had she really expected them to bring him to such a public place?

She waited, watching Dyson wait. Ten minutes. Eleven. It was as if she were waiting for a sign to let her know it was all right to go ahead with the exchange – forged document for damaged friend.

But there would be no sign. The decision had to be hers. The resolve had slipped.

Steven Dyson looked at his watch and changed posture impatiently. It was the only sign she would get. She descended the tower and walked towards him.

He smiled when he saw her.

"Toni! I'd almost given you up."

He pushed past a three-generation family who were watching the clown and embraced her. It looked like a perfectly normal greeting but it took her aback. Both his arms were round her and his right hand was inside her open cardigan.

"I have to be sure, my dear," he said quietly, the grin still in place. "Your friend has a fondness for noisy weapons."

His hand felt both her breasts and she steeled herself not to struggle. A search had been half expected but not in so public a fashion. She looked over his shoulder but no one was taking any notice.

He remained smiling when he released her and took the raffia bag from her shoulder.

"Allow me."

She attempted to step away from him but backed into somebody. More hands held her by the arms.

"Don't struggle. Smile. You're having a good time," Steven said. "You're with old friends. Say hello to Carl."

"Hello, Toni love."

Carl Curtis. The man's grip was iron. There was no point struggling.

"Toni!" A second man appeared at Dyson's shoulder. "You look smashing."

Dyson searched the bag.

"Keep smiling if you want to see Morgan. Ah." He found the gun. "Now that is naughty."

He palmed it, slipped it beneath his sweater and into the waistband of his trousers. He handed her back the raffia bag and Curtis let go of her arms.

"Where's Maudie?"

"All in good time."

"We had a deal. The contract for Maudie."

"Quite so. But not here. He's in a van. It's not far. Shall we . . . ?"

"No. Bring him here. I've brought the contract, you bring Maudie."

The grin froze on Dyson's face.

"My dear. Please don't make a scene. Carl could really hurt you if he tried." Curtis gripped her arms again.

"Now. I must insist that you come with us. Your laughing clown is getting on my nerves."

To an outsider they simply looked a part of the jostling, high-spirited crowd that wandered from one attraction to the next. She looked beyond the clown, up to the long window above the Fun House entrance. A line of teenagers was looking out, leaning on a rhythmically shuffling plank. They formed a crazy noncommittal chorus line for her abduction. They took no notice. No one was taking any notice.

She kicked backwards and her heel connected with Curtis's ankle.

"Bitch!" he hissed, and tightened his grip so that she cried out.

"Alan. Help him. Let's move her. And please, Toni. Don't make them hurt you."

Alan and Curtis flanked her. They held an arm each, their arms round her waist and shoulders, a friendly threesome, although the woman in the middle would perhaps appear to be a little loud, a little the worse for drink.

But so what? So were many others. Steven Dyson led the way.

Chapter 27

RUTH stayed off the Promenade and took the back streets, burning the road with short bursts of acceleration between the junctions. She made good time.

Maudie lay the shotgun on the back seat and covered it with the trenchcoat.

"She's meeting them at the Fun House. I want the closest entrance. Drop me and wait in the car."

"Main entrance. Go straight in, past Noah's Ark, left, up the slope. You can't miss it."

He took the Luger from his belt, checked its action and cocked it before replacing it. His leg ached like fuck and he had shooting pains in his chest. It wasn't a question of missing it, it was a question of making it.

"There," she said, turning right on to a long road of boarding-houses. The road had been reduced to a single lane by parked cars.

To the left, beyond a car park and high wall, he could see the fretwork structures of the Big Dipper, the Grand National and white-knuckle rides.

She went fast along the road, past the car park entrance, and braked outside a white circular building.

"Time?" he said, opening the door.

"Ten past nine."

He started to run and almost fell when his left leg buckled. All he could manage was a shuffling lope in which he dragged it by willpower. Quasimodo to the rescue.

The noise, lights, smells, faces and pain were a kaleidoscope. They hit his senses in a random attack. The rumble of a high-speed ride, the shrieks of its passengers, a fat woman pushing a hot dog into her mouth and mustard dribbling on her chin like seagull shit.

Past Noah's Ark and up the slope. He hurt all over and he wheezed the air into his lungs. A huge black spider spun in front of him, lifting cages of people in banked spirals. Beyond it was the Fun House.

He kept moving, his eyes searching. Anger berated his body for being so weak. The laughing clown still laughed but Toni was not there.

Too late.

Too late?

He stopped by the clown. Its laughter mocked him. His eyes bore through the crowds, willing her to be there.

The carousel. Past the carousel. He saw them. Two men holding her, walking her away. He went after them.

One of the men was Carl Curtis but the other was an unknown. There was no sign of Steven Dyson. Then he saw him – and Dyson saw Maudie.

Steven was a short distance ahead, masked by the threesome that followed. He stepped to one side and turned to speak and their eyes met.

The words were stillborn. Instead he cursed a profanity that Maudie could lip read at this distance. The threesome stopped and the two men holding Toni looked back. Toni twisted but was unable to turn her head.

They moved on, attempting to increase their pace, Toni attempting to hamper them.

Past Alice in Wonderland and, unbelievably, he was gaining and the pain did not seem so bad.

Alongside the Ghost Train a public ramp climbed to a higher level. It was narrow, people closer together, and it slowed them even more. Maudie again closed the gap.

The top of the ramp provided an open crossroad of entertainment. A doughnut bar to the left, shops, arcades and log flume to the right. They had gone straight ahead, along a raised walkway. Curtis and Toni, Dyson in front . . .

The other man?

He saw him coming from the side of the doughnut bar at the last moment. In attempting to get out of the way, he staggered and held out his left arm for support. The heavy took it gratefully, and reached for Maudie's other arm. He didn't make it.

Maudie ripped the knife free, sprang the blade and followed his stagger through by pushing it upwards into the man's body. It jolted as it chipped a rib but it went in all the way.

The young man's menace had become dead weight. Maudie supported him for a second, then let him slide off the blade. He closed it as he turned away and continued along the walkway, slipping it into his trouser pocket.

As always, it would take time before people reacted.

Another drunk.

Don't get involved.

Dyson, Curtis and Toni were twenty yards ahead. Dyson gave orders and took money out of his pocket. He thrust it through the window of a kiosk. The three of them went through a turnstile and on to an iron bridge that went across a narrow-gauge railway.

Stairs at the other side led down to the platform of a station. A train waited below, scaled-down engine and one operator, and behind, carriages straight out of toytown. Three open, one enclosed, two more open. Each had eight pairs of seats, all facing forward. The deteriorating weather meant there was only a handful of passengers.

At the turnstile the woman said, "Your friend paid."

He pushed through on to the bridge, hand going under his shirt. Curtis waited at the other end, filling it with his bulk. Below, on the platform, Steven Dyson was pushing Toni towards the rear of the train where there were no travellers.

"It's over," Curtis said.

His right hand hung casually at his side. It held a revolver, its snout extended by a silencer.

Maudie had never believed in chat for the sake of it. Chat took a fraction of concentration that could be better used on action. He held on to the bridge rail with his left hand and doubled forward to get his breath. He felt like death.

Curtis continued to talk.

"You've done well, for an old man. But now . . . "

The engine below them hooted. It drowned Curtis's words. Maudie took the gun from his waistband and shot him while it was still sounding.

The bullet hit Curtis high in the chest. It shut him up but did not knock him over. Maudie fired again but nothing happened. The damn thing had jammed. Blasted Melvyn. Blasted amateurs. He used both hands to re-cock it but a blow sent him sprawling on to his backside.

He looked along the bridge and saw that Curtis was still at the far end, his back against the steel mesh. For a moment, he was puzzled as to who had hit him. When his left arm would not work he realised he had been shot in the shoulder.

His injury rendered the Luger useless because he needed both hands to free the chamber. He dropped it on to the concrete and gripped the mesh to pull himself up. It hurt too much and he paused.

The engine below hooted again. It was an impatient sound. Toni was down there, still in danger. He had given his word and there wasn't a lot left any more but his word.

He reached out again and pulled. The pain reached a pitch where it could get no worse. It didn't matter any more. His remaining strength did.

When he was on his feet he looked at Curtis. The man appeared to be waiting patiently, leaning back against the wire wall, legs straight but no balance. The gun was still in his right hand by his side.

Maudie adjusted his own balance. His left shoulder was burning fiercely and his left side was numb. He let go of the rail and put his hand in his pocket.

"Hey, mister. You dropped your gun."

He looked round slowly. Watching with solemn eyes from the walkway were two boys, brothers. They were aged about eight and ten. It was the elder who had spoken. The younger continued to eat crisps. They had seen it all before, on television. This might be real but it wasn't new.

Further along, perhaps fifteen yards away, a girl of about eighteen also watched indifferently. Her companions had their backs to the rail and she was continuing to listen to their conversation while watching at the same time.

Perhaps she thought he was another drunk.

It was another slide for his kaleidoscope.

He turned away and walked towards Curtis. The knife, sticky with the unknown's blood, was in his hand. His left leg dragged more noticeably. His lungs were a furnace.

Curtis was alive and bleeding a lot beneath his jacket. His mouth was open but as Maudie neared he clamped it shut with effort and tried to raise the gun. His arm lifted, but not far enough. It dropped back to his side.

Maudie released the blade, held it before him from the waist, point up, and walked into him, using his body weight to push it in to the hilt.

They could have been embracing. Two inebriates full of false affection. Instead it was deadly affection. Maudie felt the man's breath gush on to his cheek. Then there was no more breath.

He pushed himself away from Curtis who, surprisingly, remained upright. Forget the knife. Probably didn't have the strength to pull it out. The gun. Take the gun.

He did so, from limp fingers.

The hooting.

The train.

It was chugging. Leaving the station. He went down the stairs, letting gravity take him, his good arm, the arm that held the gun, hooked over the rail to guide him and keep him upright. When the stairs ended, he fell on to his knees on the concrete platform.

The first open carriages had moved past him. A family in the enclosed section looked at him curiously as they went by. There were two open carriages left. He stepped closer. Dyson and Toni were the only remaining occupants. They were in the first seats of the last carriage. Dyson's eyes were wild. Toni, by his side, was distraught.

They went past him.

He jumped.

Chapter 28

THE train ran around the southern section of the Pleasure Beach perimeter. Toni had ridden it before, with her niece Lucia. It had been an animated journey and they had enjoyed the hidden villages that housed plastercast Africans and Indians and dinosaurs, and they had laughed when it skirted waterways of slow rafts or tunnelled beneath the hollow structures of other rides.

This time she had watched, in horror, the confrontation on the bridge. The detail was obscured by the girderwork but the outcome had been apparent. Maudie had been wounded. Curtis had been killed.

The train was moving when he had begun his descent of the stairs and she had lost sight of him halfway down. Then there he was. Her hired gun. Standing at the edge of the platform.

He looked wrecked. One arm dangled uselessly, the knit shirt was dark with blood. In his other hand he held a gun but did not appear to have the strength to lift it. His face was luminous, as if the blood from it had already been drained by the wound.

She sat on the inside and Steven Dyson held her left arm twisted behind her back. But now his attention was wholly fixed on the shattered figure at the end of the platform. Dyson's agitation was close to panic.

Toni prepared to duck in case Maudie fired the gun but he didn't move. They twisted on the hard wooden bench as they went past, to keep him in sight.

Maudie flung himself on board. It wasn't a jump or a leap. It wasn't a co-ordinated move. He simply flung himself at the open seats behind.

Surely he couldn't survive that, too?

Dyson pulled the Mauser automatic from the waist-band of his trousers. He held the barrel beneath her nose.

"Don't give me cause," he said.

He turned again to look over both their shoulders. Toni twisted away from Dyson to look over her left shoulder. The raffia bag fell from her right shoulder on to her knee and she held it with her free right hand.

Where was Maudie?

The gun appeared first, clenched in his fist. He was eight seats back, at the very end of the train. He had only just made it.

"Bastard! Bastard, bastard, bastard."

Dyson levelled the gun but it wouldn't fire. He looked at it in disbelief.

Maudie's shoulder appeared, the arm moving to get a better grip. Then his head, the paleness of his face now smeared dark with blood from a gash on the temple.

He kept on coming, rising up to his feet as if he wanted to stand to make a speech. He was almost upright, and Toni began to worry about the low bridges that lay ahead, when he toppled forward into the next open seat.

It was zombi determination. His limbs were not capable of climbing so he was falling from one seat to the next.

Seven back.

Toni felt along the spine of the raffia bag to find the blunt end of the steel knitting needle she had hidden there before leaving the house. She began to withdraw it, using thumb and forefinger of her gloved right hand.

The arm reappeared on the back of the next seat. Again it was followed by a shoulder and then his head.

He paused. His eyes lost their glazed concentration for a moment and locked on hers.

He smiled. Incredibly, he smiled.

Beside her, she felt Dyson stiffen.

Maudie stood up again, and fell forward again, into the next seat.

Six away. Eighteen feet.

Dyson let go of her arm.

"One move and you're dead, bitch."

His fingers fumbled at the safety catch of the gun.

Her fingers pulled the steel needle free.

He turned, holding the gun in both hands, waiting for Maudie to reappear.

Maudie's fist, still clutching the silenced revolver, came into sight.

Dyson was breathing through his mouth. In his eagerness, he was leaning forward, one knee on the seat.

Toni turned to look over her right shoulder so that the needle was between their bodies and pointing at Dyson. She cushioned the blunt end with a small pack of tissues in her right palm.

Behind her, Maudie's shoulder was slowly appearing. Dyson sucked in his breath in anticipation. She dropped her head, pointed the needle with her left hand, and thrust.

It went into the side of his stomach three inches and stuck. Damn it, it stuck.

He screamed and half stood in surprise. The needle protruded from him like an arrow. He stared at it in horror, then at her.

He raised the gun and pointed it at her face. She looked at the end of the barrel. Guns kill, Maudie had said. They're deadly weapons. They kill.

She waited on a toytown ride through a pleasure park to be killed.

And then it wasn't there any more. The side of

Dyson's head exploded and he and the gun flipped backwards out of the train as they went beneath the white timbers of the Big Dipper.

Toni looked back. Maudie hung over the back of a seat, held by his right arm, the revolver still pointing.

She climbed over to join him.

Chapter 29

IT wasn't over yet and the knowledge bothered Maudie. Toni was still a problem. She was there, trying to make him comfortable.

She was saying his name, murmuring her concern, vehemently declaring he would be all right.

He smiled and allowed her to straighten him into a sitting position on the seat, despite the pain.

The train continued to rumble on its way, the engine hooting. People beyond it, in the gloom and flashing neon, continued to laugh and shriek in fun.

Toni cradled his head and began to cry. He didn't want her to cry. Not here. Not yet. He struggled to sit up properly.

"No tears, gel. Still things to do. You've got to get clear before the police arrive."

She stopped crying and looked at him.

"We've got to get clear, Maudie. I'm not going anywhere without you."

"Now don't be stupid, gel. I'm in no fit state."

His words steeled her.

"We go together or we don't go at all."

"Listen. The Dysons are done for. You're in the clear."

"Maudie. You listen. I'm not leaving you. If I leave you, it's all been for nothing. I did everything like you said. I wore gloves. We're both in the clear. We're both going."

He laughed. The pain wasn't too bad now. Either that

or it had stopped registering. He just felt incapable of moving.

"You're a headstrong girl, Toni Rossetti, and we made a lovely team. But you don't know when you're beat."

"Neither do you. And that's why you're too precious to leave on a train to nowhere."

He shook his head in exasperation and to shake away the tears he felt threatening.

"I can't walk, Toni."

"You can lean on me."

"And how far do you think we'll get?"

"As far as we need to." She was fervent. "You're coming with me, Maudie. If I have to drag you."

He realised she was not going to be dissuaded. It meant reorganising his thoughts. He looked at the gun. He had planned to use it on himself. Anything, he felt, was preferable to going back inside. But now, Toni's determination meant he would have to risk that possibility. He dropped the gun out of the carriage.

"We'll give it a go, gel."

She kissed his cheek before taking off her cardigan.

"This will hide the blood on your shirt."

She helped him to put his right arm into the sleeve but his left was useless and she draped the rest of the garment over his wounded shoulder.

"Where does this bleedin' train go to?" he asked.

"Back to where we started."

He chuckled at the irony.

"That's about bleedin' par for the course."

"When it gets to the station, we get off on to a different platform. There's an exit close to where we'll stop. There are still plenty of people about, plenty of drunks. If you stagger, it won't be noticed."

He nodded.

"Ruth brought me," he said. "She's waiting with a car at the main entrance. By the round, white building. If we can make it that far."

"We'll make it."

Maudie was not too sure. Much more exertion and he would pass out and she wouldn't be able to carry him alone. He also knew she wouldn't walk away if he did. Christ. He would just have to make sure he didn't pass out.

"We're nearly there," she said, and the train slowed round the last bend as it came back into the station.

On the bridge at the far end of the platform a group of people had gathered round the body of Carl Curtis. They were indecisive and appeared to be waiting for the police. That was good. If the law wasn't here yet, there was still a chance.

Toni was right. The carriage stopped almost alongside the exit. With her help he got out. She pulled his right arm around her shoulder and they walked slowly through the gate.

The pain had returned with the movement and he felt so weak he wondered how he could stand. He knew he was leaning heavily on Toni but she was taking the strain and forcing him to match her paces.

"We have to go up," she said.

They climbed steps. He didn't know how many, just that there were too many. It felt like Everest. When they finished they were at the crossroad at the top of the ramp where Maudie had dealt with the heavy.

A semicircle of holidaymakers faced the doughnut stand, strangely silent. Those at the back craned over shoulders for a glimpse of death. A youth continued to eat chips while he looked, then turned to exchange an excited but muted comment with a friend.

Thunder rumbled and the sky darkened. They headed down the ramp but after only a few yards he knew he couldn't last much longer. The first heavy drops of rain fell and people began to run for shelter, jostling them so that they had to stop, Toni taking virtually all his weight as he clung to the side of the ramp.

"It's no good, gel. I've had it."

"Damn you, Maudie. I'm not going to lose you, too. Try, you old sod. Try."

He tried and they made it to the bottom of the ramp. They staggered on and he saw Alice in Wonderland statues and wondered whether they were real or if he was hallucinating.

They could do with a white rabbit, to carry him to safety. A white rabbit or a hole in the ground down which he could fall without effort and find undisturbed sleep.

Toni moved and was replaced by a powerful arm that lifted him virtually off his feet. They began to cover the ground quickly. In his confused state he still thought of white rabbits and when he turned to look, he half expected to see whiskers and pointed ears.

It was no rabbit. It was Stuart Shapiro. They were going to make it.

Epilogue

THREE WEEKS LATER

BLACKPOOL Railway Station seemed an appropriate place to say goodbye.

Maudie and Toni stood away from the flow of passengers that pushed through the ticket barriers and headed for the waiting train. He wore his dry-cleaned lightweight suit and the sunglasses whose lenses adapted to the light. The Samsonite case, containing the rest of his clothes and the pump-action shotgun, was at his feet.

He was travelling first class back to Euston and a taxi ride to the Tout's bedsit in Brick Lane.

Maudie remembered little of the days that immediately followed the shoot-out at the Pleasure Beach. Stuart Shapiro, alerted on his car telephone by Ruth, had arrived on schedule to make it a fairytale ending that quickly became Lewis Carroll.

Instead of a registered medical practitioner, the market baron obtained the services of a Pakistani entrepreneur from Blackburn whose Rawalpindi doctorate had not been recognised by the British Medical Association. He visited Maudie frequently in a van marked Shabnam Knitwear and told him tales of commonplace bullet wounds on the North West Frontier.

A hospital would have meant life on the inside. Dr Ali was a chance of life on the outside. It worked.

Maudie's presence at a hospital would also have been unwelcome to the police, who, after suffering apoplexy at the wholesale killings, went looking for a quick solution to reassure holidaymakers there would be no more. Their investigations revealed the unsavoury Manchester links that Eric and Steven Dyson had had and which provided background for any number of theories. But they chose the one that fitted: the Scottish connection.

Bouncers at The Life of Riley no longer felt the same constraints or bravado now that Unsworth, Curtis and the Dysons were not there. They told the police that the two Manchester professionals, along with Graham and Melvyn, had been responsible for beating the boys from Stirling so badly that one had died and another was still critical.

Supportive evidence was found in the club's car park. The word SCOTLAND had been scrawled in capital letters along the side of Eric Dyson's Rover motor car. One of the chefs also said he thought the man with the shotgun had had a Scottish accent. It was amazing what fear prompted people to say, Maudie reflected.

The surviving Scots didn't argue with the hypothesis. They were pleased their enemies had received terminal retribution and were disinclined to deny that a heavy mob had travelled south on their behalf to mete out justice. After all, it did their image the world of good.

"I'll see you soon, Maudie. Promise," Toni said. "When I get back from the States."

"You sure you're coming back?"

"I'm sure. And this time it's for good."

The people who moved past them with impatient strides and purposeful expressions seemed like extras in their drama.

"When you get back, do as Stuart says. Find a proper chap."

"I found one but he says he's too old."

He laughed.

"Too bloody true, gel."

"Will you come back?"

"Maybe. But not for a while."

Toni and Mario had urged him to stay and had offered a directorship in the business. It had been tempting but too many people had seen his face. If they saw it again, it might revive memories.

At least cash was going to be no problem for a while. They had increased his fee and he had £25,000 in readies stitched into the inside pocket of his jacket. Brick Lane was going to be a temporary stop. He thought he might try Southend and look for that well-preserved widow he had promised himself.

"It's goodbye time, Toni."

"Yes."

They embraced and she sighed.

"No tears, now," he warned.

"No tears." She sniffed them back. "Thanks, Maudie."

"Thank you, gel. Take care."

He released her, took his ticket from his top pocket, picked up the case and went through the barrier.

He didn't look back. He'd had enough of looking back. For the first time in years, he felt he had a future.

IAN RANKIN

KNOTS AND CROSSES

It's frightening . . . And in Edinburgh of all places, I mean, you never think of that sort of thing happening in Edinburgh, do you?

Already two young girls have been abducted and killed. Now a third is missing. Nothing in common between them: different areas, different circumstances. A random killer.

Polite, self-regarding Edinburgh is in a state of shock. All police leave is cancelled; the reporters gather like vultures.

Meanwhile Detective Sergeant John Rebus, smoking and drinking too much, his wife gone taking their own young daughter, has another, more personal puzzle on his hands. Someone is sending him taunting, anonymous letters with little pieces of knotted string and matchstick crosses.

Annoying but hardly important. Not when a cold, methodical killer is stalking the frightened streets . . .

'Quite brilliant and enormously compelling'

Martyn Goff

ANDREW COBURN

LOVE NEST

Melody was delightful. People fell in love with her. Cynics became sentimental. She was beautiful, young, enticing and heart-warming. She'd arrived in town from who knows where. Andover, Massachusetts wasn't a big place. In spite of all the recent changes and new developments, it was still a place where most people knew most people. So Melody, alluring, will-'o-the-wisp Melody, was soon known and befriended.

There were two other things about Melody.

She was a call girl, working from the Silver Bell Motor Lodge, out near Interstate 93.

And now she was dead. Murdered.

Police Sergeant Sonny Dawson, who'd loved her alive, mourned her dead – and then sadly, determinedly, set out to unravel an increasingly nasty web of small town deceit and shame.

'Combines an eye for detail with a real narrative skill'
The Times

'A marvellously accomplished thriller, full of psychological perception and sombre irony'
The London Evening Standard

K. C. CONSTANTINE

UPON SOME MIDNIGHTS CLEAR

It's Christmas time in Rocksburg, Pennsylvania, but the goodwill spirit does not affect everyone. Police chief Mario Balzic finds himself investigating a nasty mugging and an alleged theft . . . presents he and the town can do without.

'Bristles with the stuff of life, the dialogue spurts like Old Faithful'

The Observer

'Allows us to view an essentially rotten world with sympathy and understanding but without any sentimentality. Constantine started out good and just keeps getting better and better'

Time Out

'Great dialogue and an atmosphere you could cut with a coal shovel . . . an ear for dialogue that matches George V. Higgins'

Times Literary Supplement

'The sum of the parts crackles with veracity, subtlety, wit and life'

The Times

HODDER AND STOUGHTON PAPERBACKS

LES ROBERTS

AN INFINITE NUMBER OF MONKEYS

Saxon was in when the phone rang.

He was in a lot these nights. Mostly just watching his house plant die of causes unknown and mourning the departure of the most recent love of his life.

Plus, as an actor he was resting and as a private eye he was between engagements.

The woman on the line was slim, good-looking, brunette. He could tell. His secretary, Jo. A terrified Jo. Someone had just taken a pot-shot at her husband. Which was odd, considering Marsh Zeidler was Mr Inoffensive USA.

But then it turned out that he was doing some stuff with Buck Weldon. Who was a very rich man with a list of enemies longer than many of his bestselling stories.

Saxon was about to get involved in a plot where the truth was as strange, as complicated and a good deal nastier than anything in Buck Weldon's fiction.

HODDER AND STOUGHTON PAPERBACKS